THE MERMAID'S LAMENT

SHAY GREEN, BOOK ONE

ALEXES RAZEVICH

RAZOR STREET PUBLISHING

Copyright © 2019 Alexes Razevich

All rights reserved

This is a work of fiction. Names, characters, places, and incidents either are the products of the author's imagination or are used fictionally. Any resemblance to actual events, locals, organizations, or persons, living or dead, is entirely coincidently and beyond the intent of either the author or the publisher.

All rights reserved. No part of this publication may be reproduced or transmitted in any form or by any means, electronic or mechanical, including photography, recording, or any information storage and retrieval system without permission in writing from the author. Requests for permission should be sent to Lxsraz@yahoo.com.

❀ Created with Vellum

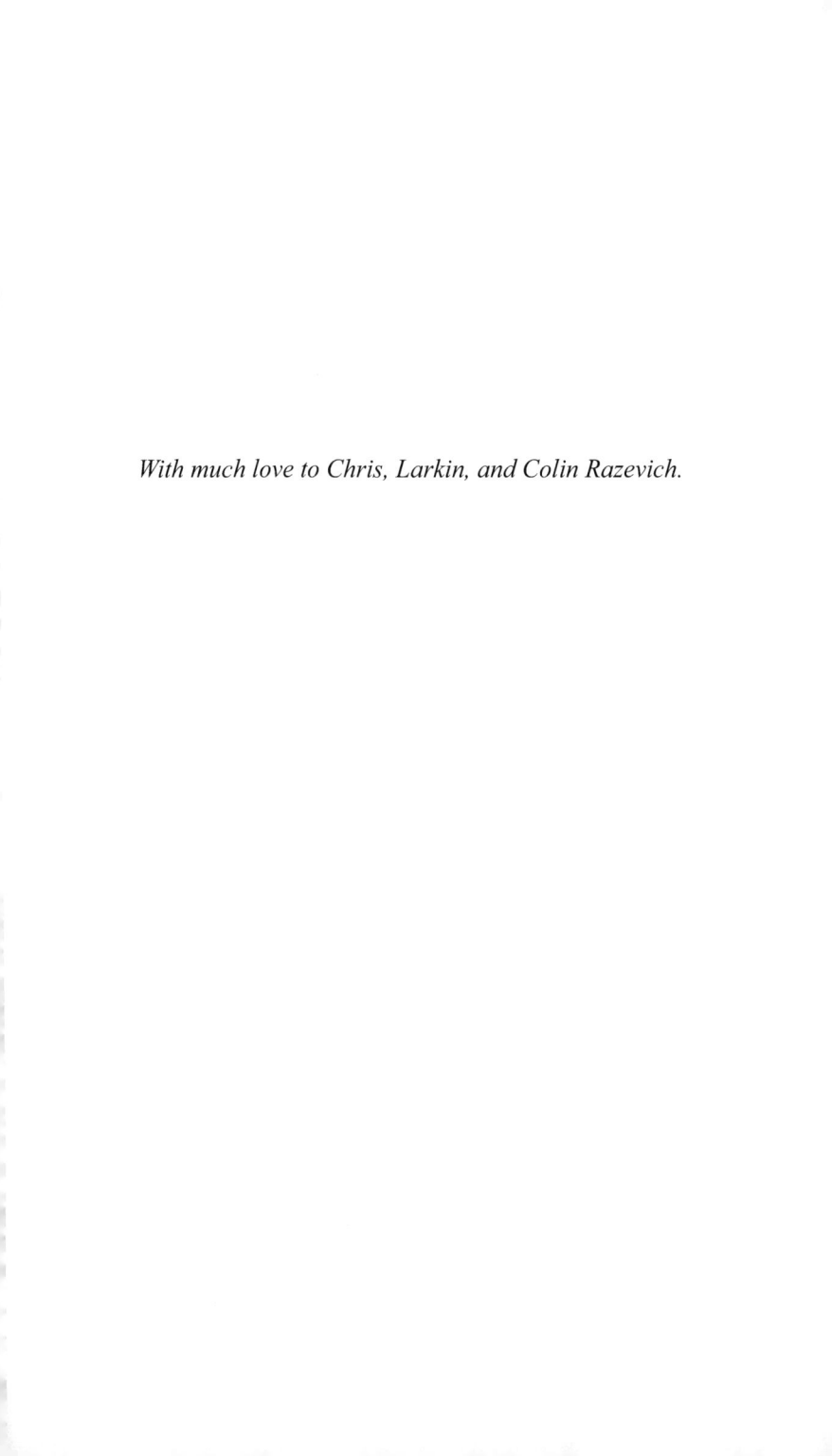

With much love to Chris, Larkin, and Colin Razevich.

1

The demon burst through the doors cursing like a marine and reeking of patchouli oil.

There were seven women in the reception area of the penthouse office suite—me, and five others whom were vying for the job of companion to entrepreneur Lady Califia, founder and CEO of Zubris Enterprises.

Except that, according to the friend who'd told me about the opening, *companion* was a euphemism for 'Lady isn't saying what specific job she wants done until the person is hired.' I've worked for secretive clients before. It wasn't that unusual in my line of work: rescue and recovery.

The seventh person was a very young-looking receptionist who was pointing at the demon and screaming loud enough to raise the dead.

I was on my feet in half a heartbeat, taking in the demon's particulars, trying to match it with something—anything—I'd faced before or had heard about, looking for the best way to bring it down.

Every inch of the demon's eight or so feet was warty green skin. Random sprouts of hair as thick and the same color as broomstick straw stuck out from its face. Its muscle-bound arms looked steroid built. The wrists were thick and the hands big enough to easily wrap over a basketball. Its feet were long and broad, good for balance, and ended in wicked looking talons.

Was it like anything I'd seen before?

Nope.

All the job seekers had leaped to their feet, some with weapons drawn, each woman set in her fighting stance. I readied a casting to halt the demon in place, visualizing in my mind what I wanted my chosen element to do. As a made-elemental, I had fire, water, air, and earth available, and had decided on air.

The demon had bee lined for the receptionist's ultra-modern chrome and bamboo desk, reached across and hauled the screaming blonde girl—she couldn't have been more than seventeen, eighteen—out of her chair as though she were no heavier or studier than a rag doll. Before I could get my casting off, the demon slung the receptionist over its shoulder and held her in place with a massive, warty, green hand. The demon hustled out the door with the kind of amazing speed I'd only seen in vampires.

I jetted after them, my mind busy with plans. I'd checked the floor's layout when I'd gotten off the elevator, standard practice for me. There were stairs at the end of the hallway, my bet for how the demon would carry her down if abduction was his goal. Taking the elevator made no sense. The hallway was long but not so long that my casting wouldn't have its intended effect.

Except the hallway was empty. How the demon had disappeared in the mere seconds it had taken to jump to my feet and follow it out of the office and into the hallway was beyond me.

The other jobseekers had also run into the hallway. We exchanged quick, mystified glances. Three of the women fanned out—one going right of the office door, and two racing toward the door marked *Stairs*. The remaining two stood behind me as if waiting to see what I'd do before making their own decisions.

I glanced right, left, up, and down, looking for possible escape routes. Nothing in the ceiling. I couldn't see any way for the demon to have reached the stairs at the far end, even with the hellish speed it possessed. There weren't any windows for the demon to have leaped through. But there was a door to, presumably, another suite of offices down and to my left. I ran to the door, grabbed the knob and twisted it.

Locked.

One of the two women who'd followed me also reached out and tried the door. It didn't open for her either.

Because no one was at work there today? Because whoever rented the suite didn't want just anyone walking in? Or because the demon had thought it a useful hiding place and had locked the door behind it?

I readied myself to blow the door open with a stormworthy blast of air but heard a click before I set the blast free —the door unlocking. I stood a moment, trying to feel if it was a trap.

The door was pulled open. The receptionist beamed at me. I looked over her head into the room. There was no sign of the demon.

"Shall we?" she said cheerfully and skipped across the hall back toward the offices like a happy child with her basket full of posies.

"Trick," one of the women who'd followed me muttered.

I nodded, irritated but intrigued by this show. There was a point to this, I was sure, but what that point was, eluded me.

"It's over," I called toward the women who'd fanned out earlier. "She's fine."

The receptionist waved toward them, calling out, "Everything's okay. Please come back inside."

When we'd all returned to the office, the receptionist flashed a smile and gave us a wink as she pranced through the room and once again ensconced herself behind her desk.

Pissed off mutterings of '*Shit*' and '*Well, fuck,*' darkened the room as the realization that the abduction was staged broke over the applicants who hadn't already figured it out. I took note of who carried what weapons as the women put away throwing stars, knives, and guns.

Who comes to a job interview armed like that? Evidently, everyone but me. But then, I was a made-elemental. I carried my arsenal inside myself, always ready when I needed it. These women weren't garden variety bodyguards or anything else either. I felt magic swirling around in each one.

What confused me was the demon. Why would someone *ordin*—a non-magical person—which I assumed Lady Califia was, fake a demon attack? True, she'd evidently specified a magical for this job, which was unusual but not unheard of in the *ordin* world, especially for someone of Lady Califia's wealth. Money buys a lot of things. Knowledge of hidden worlds among them. And, evidently, rent-a-demons.

I shifted my attention back to the receptionist. She was all business now, walking around the room handing each applicant a clipboard with a blank, lined piece of paper on it, and a Montblac ballpoint pen. *Montblanc*. Very nice.

"If you will each write down what you just saw," she said, "that would be lovely. No conferring with others. Sign your name at the bottom."

There was a quick bit of we applicants glancing at each other in a *What's going on here*? way before we bent over our tasks. Other than irritation at having been suckered in by the fake demon abduction, no one seemed the least bit thrown off by the theatrics we'd witnessed. We were all professionals, by the looks of things. From what I'd heard about Lady Califia, she'd accept no less.

Lady wasn't her title, it was her first name, and she was beyond wealthy. I wasn't sure numbers went as high as her net worth. She'd made it all herself, which I appreciated. Or rather, she'd found a treasure and turned it into a thriving enterprise.

Lady Califia had been thirty-three, only a year older than I was now, when she found the sunken *Pride of Zubis* and recovered the treasure in its hold. In the seven years since, she'd taken the initial find and built an empire around it.

There was the theme park that everyone wanted to go to, the imitation crown and jewels that every little girl just had to have in her princess closet, the replica Sword of Zubis that every young (and quite a number of teen) boy craved. A few adult men also had the replica sword hanging in their living rooms or bedrooms; I knew this from seeing social media posts from grown-ass Zubis-nerds.

Each to their own, I say.

Lady Califia ran her empire from this penthouse office suite at the Cooper Building in downtown Los Angeles, where we would-be companions now waited to be called for our one-on-one interviews. After the demon charade, I was rather looking forward to the one-on-one which I hoped would be with Ms. Califia herself and not just some minion. I had questions for the entrepreneur, starting with *What the hell was that demon crap about?*

When the last of the applicants looked up, indicating she'd finished writing down what she'd seen, the receptionist collected the clipboards and pens back into the same cardboard box she'd drawn them from. She sat back in her black Aeron chair and beamed at us as if we were children who had just managed to tie their shoelaces semi-well for the first time. I don't know what the other applicants did in response, but I simply stared at her, the blandest expression I could muster plastered on my face.

The receptionist broke off her beaming in our direction and began reading our 'witness statements,' separating them into two piles. I figured the piles were the 'reject' and the 'second step' groups.

The baby receptionist picked up one pile, rose from her chair, and went to a tall oak door with an intricately inscribed gold knob paired with a deco design black and gold back plate. Ms. Califia seemed to spare no expense, and she had good taste. The receptionist opened the door and disappeared behind it. I didn't think that was Lady's private office. Most execs liked to be a bit removed from the hoi polloi that regularly came into reception areas—salesmen, break room service people, and the like.

I got up to look closely at the doorknob.

"Runes?" one of the other applicants asked.

I nodded as I let my eyes go unfocused and sensed the door. Under the dark-brown stain, the entire thing was covered in runes.

"Really?" another applicant said. "What sort?"

"Protection," I said. Evidently, I wasn't the only one who seemed surprised that magic was in use here.

I sensed someone approaching from the other side of the runed door and casually made my way back to my seat.

The baby receptionist opened the door and stepped back into the reception area, accompanied by a tall, brown-skinned man with luxurious black hair. I guessed he was East Indian or Pakistani, that part of the world at least. Magic visibly radiated from him in lines, like one of those Our Lady of Guadalupe paintings. I was pretty sure he didn't walk around the streets like that and wondered why he wanted to make his magic so obvious to us. And who, or what, the richest woman in the country really was.

Baby receptionist held up a list she had in her hands.

"As I call your name, please stand," she said.

Two names were called. Mine—Shay Greene—wasn't among them. Disappointment sidled through me. Not that I desperately needed the job—I didn't, but the whole situation was . . .odd, and, frankly, I was curious.

The receptionist eyed the standing women, as if taking their measure. Maybe she had some bet with herself about who would make the final cut. The tall man with the lovely mane of hair stared slightly over the standing applicant's heads, his face a masque of disinterest. I say a masque because the magic that had radiated off him in spokes now undulated like dancing snakes. I was pretty sure that was a sign of intense, not *dis*, interest.

"Thank you," the receptionist said to the standing applicants. "I just need you to sign these non-disclosure agreements. Your parking stubs can be validated at the front desk downstairs."

It took a moment for the standing women to realize they were being dismissed. The looks of excited expectation they had worn shifted to display their own disappointment. The rest of us watched silently as each woman signed the agreement and headed out the door.

When the last of the rejects had left, the receptionist cast her glance over the remaining four applicants; all of who—me included—had figured out we'd made the cut. "If you will kindly follow Doctor Sharma, he will lead you to the interview room."

2

We four followed Dr. Sharma down a long, white hallway wide enough for all of us to walk side-by-side. White globes that hung a couple of inches below the high ceiling lit the hall. I was third in line behind a woman I'd describe as 'strapping.' She was tall, six feet or so, muscular with the lean muscles of a runner or soccer player and dressed throat to ankle in leather as black as her hair.

Dr. Sharma hustled ahead and opened another oak door.

"Son of a bitch!" Leather Woman cried and spun to send Dr. Sharma a glare so hot it could melt glass. "Do you think we're stupid? That door is protected. Opened or closed, any stranger trying to cross the threshold is in for a nasty surprise."

I let my eyes go unfocused and saw pulsing, neon-orange ward lines crisscrossing the door and jamb. Strong wards, powerful enough to have thrown Leather Woman into the wall behind us if she'd tried to enter the room before they were disarmed.

There was more to it than just wards, though. I was sure

of that. I opened my senses to feel for what else was going on and blew out a breath when I got it.

"Who here is a curse breaker?" I said. "Anyone?"

I didn't hold out a lot of hope. Curse breakers were a rare commodity since curse throwers tended to hunt them down and kill them. Curse throwers are a nasty bunch.

A seriously short, thin woman, maybe mid-twenties, with short, spiky brown hair and dressed in an almost knee-length forest-green sweater over brown leggings stepped up. She couldn't have looked more 'wood sprite' if she'd had pointy ears. I had my reasons for not trusting the fae and was glad this woman's ears showed her to be human.

"I'm a curse breaker," she said.

I turned to her. "Can you do something about the curse on this door?"

She regarded the door a moment, tilting her head left and then right, as if getting a bead on the curse.

"Not much of a curse here, honestly. A little pinch will do." She reached into the brown leather purse she carried, inclining her head down to see inside. "Now where is that? Ah."

She pulled out a small, round, silver tin surrounded by a purple haze of wards. She muttered some words to clear off the wards. When the wards had dissipated, melting away like dew in the sun, she opened the tin, gathered a pinch of something vegetative and blue—dried flowers maybe?—and rolled it between her thumb and first two fingers.

"Move back," she said, her voice suddenly firm and authoritative. Leather Woman and I backed up to stand with the other applicant who leaned against the wide hallway's far wall.

She tossed the crumbs toward the door. The curse broke

as if the delicate flower bits were rocks shattering glass. I was impressed.

Leather Woman stepped forward, seemingly determined to be first through the door after all. I grabbed her arm to stop her.

"I wouldn't do that," I said. "There's more than a curse and some wards guarding this door."

"Pftt," the curse breaker noised. "It's a secondary curse and it's mostly for show." She wriggled her fingers and muttered a few words. Her voice came back to normal and she said, "All done. We can go in now."

I shook my head. "There's something else going on here, but I can't quite tell what."

Leather Woman gave a dismissive sort of snort and strode through the open doorway. Nothing hit her, or jumped out, or in any way seemed designed to further keep us from entering the room. I scratched my head as the curse breaker followed Leather Woman into the room. Something else was definitely at work here, but evidently it wasn't anything designed to stop us. I stepped through the doorway.

A frizz of *something* prickled over my skin as I passed through the jambs into the room. The door slammed shut.

"Sorting door," I said, now that the *something else* I'd felt had made itself known.

Leather Woman gave the curse breaker and me the once over. "Either we're selected or rejected. My bet is on selected."

I thought so, too. We were the three who'd taken charge. A thrill of anticipation ran up my breastbone.

Dr. Sharma clapped his hands to get our attention. "Congratulations. One of you will be offered the position of companion to Lady Califia."

Great. Were we going to arm-wrestle each other, and the winner got the job?

As if he'd heard my thoughts, Dr. Sharma said, "As you know, Ms. Califia is a powerful, wealthy woman. As you might have guessed, that sort of position engenders jealousy, greed, and threats to her well-being. She needs to know that whomever she selects for the position is able to protect her physically. To that end, she requests a demonstration of your skills."

Criminy. We *were* going to arm-wrestle. Or some equivalent of that. Probably a rather more aggressive equivalent. I hoped we weren't really about to be asked to fight each other. I was growing a little fond of Leather Woman and Curse Breaker. I wouldn't want to hurt them just to get a job.

I glanced around the large room. It reminded me of what I imagined a Victorian Men's Club might have looked like. Dark wood paneling. Long, thin windows with heavy, gold draperies. Thick, expensive-looking rugs over dark oak floors. Comfy-looking, maroon, wingback chairs set around dark wood side tables, the groupings close enough together to not make the room look weird but far enough apart that each little assemblage could hold private conversations if people kept their voices low.

Five identical doors with brass doorknobs broke up the expanse of the room's far wall. Leather Woman and Curse Breaker, I noticed, were giving the space the same sort of thoughtful once-over and both now had their gazes on the doors.

"Five doors," Dr. Sharma said, his voice taking on a grave 'movie trailer voiceover' tone, "and three of you. You will choose your door one at a time, but no one may select a door already chosen."

Which meant we weren't going to fight each other, unless

the doors all lead into the same room on the other side. Most likely we were going to duke it out with some stranger. Or some strange thing.

I was changing my mind about Lady Califia. She might or might not be magical herself, but she certainly knew our world and made use of it. But why?

That was a question for later. My immediate concern was what might be behind those doors.

Dr. Sharma nodded to me, indicating I got to be the first to choose.

I thought for a moment and then strode forward to the middle door. The knob, I noticed, was inscribed with magical symbols. The sting of a containment spell raced through my hand and up my arm when I took hold of the knob. Whatever was behind that door, no one wanted it getting out. Or they wanted to be sure that once I was inside, I couldn't get out. Neither option made me very happy.

I turned the knob and pulled the door open wide in hopes that I and my two rivals for the job (because I'm generous that way) might get a sneak peek at what lay beyond. All I saw was a child sized figure hunkered down at the far end of a space so long and narrow it was more like a shaft than a proper room. The figure was sitting on the floor, bent over with its back to me. I couldn't tell if it was male or female, human or something else.

I took two steps into the room and halted, waiting, letting whomever or whatever was in there with me make the first move. The clunk of the door firmly shutting startled me and I flinched.

The person/creature in the corner didn't move for a long moment, but finally began to unwind, growing larger as it did —its chambray-clad back rising first, its shaggy-haired blond head following. My opponent rose to standing using leg-strength alone. I swallowed, plenty impressed by that.

Even before the creature turned around, I'd decided it was male but probably not human. If human, he was misshapen—his thick, muscular arms too long for normal, his back also too long and too wide, his powerfully built legs, encased in blue jeans, a bit too short. All in all, I guessed him to be about six and a half feet tall, nearly a foot taller than me, but our legs were about the same length. I dearly regretted not bringing a weapon with me today. I certainly hadn't expected a test like this at a job interview.

Well then, magic would just have to do.

He turned around, displaying a hard-edged but bumpy face with deep-set dark brown eyes and sharp, pointed upper teeth protruding over a thin lower lip. The creature's only smell was a vague scent of unwashed body, more 'gym after a workout' than 'denizen from the depths of Hell.'

"Nice clothes," I said casually. "Jeans, a chambray shirt, and cowboy boots. Not usual demon-wear."

I wondered if the cowboy boots were steel toed. That could be a problem.

The creature opened its maw, roared, and stalked toward me. I backed up the few steps available before my back touched the door. The demon had his arms flung out wide—the better to grab and squeeze me with, I figured.

I stayed where I was, back against the wall, as if frozen with fear. The creature roared again, spraying spittle on the top of my head—which was seriously gross—and snapped his arms inward to clamp them around my body. As his arms swung together, I dropped down into a crouch. The creature's arms closed around empty air above my head. I punched upward landed a good blow where his testicles would be if he were human.

Something soft and squishy was there. The creature leaned back slightly and roared again, with pain this time. I propelled myself back up to standing, put both of my palms on his stomach, and shoved as hard as I could. The creature staggered back three or four steps before catching his balance.

Pain and anger had turned his brown eyes a flaming red. He roared again. I was privileged to get a good whiff of serious halitosis.

"Toothpaste and mouthwash, dude," I said. "They really help."

Evidently he didn't appreciate my comment because he roared again and lunged toward me. This needed to be over with. I summoned up my will and sent a blast of air strong enough to knock him back half-way down the twenty-five-foot length of the room. I walked toward him and sent another blast before he could recover from the first. This blast sent him all the way to the rear of the room where he slammed against the back wall.

I focused my elemental magic and produced a rain cloud in the middle of the room. I considered throwing in some lightning for good measure but decided it would be overkill. The look of fear on the creature's face told me he knew what I'd conjured and what I intended to do with it.

I blew the cloud slowly in his direction while keeping a steady blast of air on his body so he couldn't advance toward me. The creature flattened himself against the wall as best as he could. Not that it would do him any good once the rain started falling. Working two elements at once, wind and water, isn't easy. I dropped the wind and let a small drizzle leak from the cloud. The demon screamed and the door flew open.

"That is enough!"

Dr. Sharma's voice was pitched low and loud.

I made a grabbing motion with my hand and the cloud vanished.

"Did I win?" I asked, not turning around but keeping my eyes on the demon.

Dr. Sharma raced past me, throwing a hard glance my way as he passed, and knelt beside the creature. The two spoke low to each other and I couldn't make out the words.

It dawned on me that the creature never meant to defeat me. His task was to make me show my stuff. He'd done a good job of that.

It occurred to me, too, that neither demon was necessarily what they seemed. I was beginning to suspect they were humans working under a glamour. Demons were notoriously unreliable and tended to do whatever they felt like. Why chance things going wrong if you could simply cast a glamour and make people believe they were dealing with demons?

Dr. Sharma rose to his feet and walked back over to me, speaking as he passed me heading for the open door. "If you'll come this way."

3

I followed Dr. Sharma back into the reception area and then down a different hallway with pale gray walls and plush, steel-gray carpeting underfoot that felt like walking on clouds. None of that tightly looped, hardwearing Berber for Lady Califia. Or those God-awful carpet squares that could be removed and replaced should someone grind dirt into or spill something onto them. This suite of offices spoke softly but firmly of wealth and taste.

What looked like original oil paintings broke up the long expanse of hallway. Lady's, or someone else's, preference seemed to run to California landscapes. I recognized the angled jut of Vasquez Rocks, which had stood in for an alien planet in many a TV show and movie, Mt. Shasta with a spaceship-shaped cloud resting on its summit, and Mono Lake with its massive limestone formations poking from the water. It seemed probable that all the paintings were of California natural landmarks. I wondered where the ones that weren't familiar to me were located.

At the end of the hall was a taller and wider than normal door. An *executive door* if I ever saw one. No nameplate or title designation showed whose office this was, but it was easy to guess. Dr. Sharma stopped, muttered spell-words under his breath, then turned the knob and opened the door. He stepped aside, indicating that I was to go in alone.

I recognized Lady Califia immediately. Her face was as famous and familiar as Bill Gates' or Elon Musk's. She sat behind a lovely, antique mahogany desk that I'd classify as 'regulation worker-bee sized.' No giant desk to proclaim her importance to the world. That was interesting. She looked up from where she was tapping something into a laptop computer and gave me the once over.

I gave her a moment to look, and then surveyed the office and her, getting in quick impressions to be considered in depth later.

The office was large, maybe 20x20 feet, with pale sage green walls. Persian rugs lay scattered over the dark hardwood floors. The rugs felt old to me, their age percolating slowly up from the soles of my feet. Large windows on two walls showed to-die-for views of downtown Los Angeles. More original oils of California landscapes tastefully broke up the space on the two windowless walls. She definitely had a strong preference in the art she surrounded herself with.

Lady herself looked much like she did in the photos one saw of her either breaking ground on a new project, hosting or attending charity events, or the ubiquitous headshot used in articles about her. For all that I'd seen dozens of photographs of her, she had a look that couldn't be easily categorized for heritage.

One glance at me with my pale skin, a few freckles that still hadn't faded with age, pale blue eyes, and hair that used to be strawberry blonde before it changed to silver-gray, and it's pretty obvious my ancestors come from about as far west as you can go in Europe.

Lady had skin that was not quite as coppery as Native Americans and not as dark as Creole, a wide face with high cheekbones and a strong chin. Her deep brown eyes seemed to see the heavens and the depths of hell, and into your soul while she was at it. Her hair was black, straight, cut simply and well, and fell just south of her chin. She could have been Pakistani or Iranian for all I knew but was probably mixed race. It only occurred to me now that in the articles I'd read about her before coming here today, no mention of her parents was ever made.

She wore little make up beyond lip gloss and was dressed in a simple black sheath dress cut impeccably well. A red linen jacket hung on a hanger on a peg near the door. A small, black leather handbag hung on a peg next to the jacket. To see her shoes, I'd have had to bend down and peeked under the desk, but my bet would be they were black and expensive.

I felt downright dowdy in comparison.

"Tell me about your background," Lady said, forgoing any pleasantries. "And how you make your living."

There were two armchairs upholstered in blue leather in front of her desk, but she hadn't invited me to sit. Power stance or rudeness? Not that there was a lot of difference between the two.

"My specialty is rescue and recovery," I said. "I'm very good at finding lost people and missing things and bringing them home."

Lady nodded. "Who are *your* people?"

Funny that she would ask me the exact question I'd wondered about her. I cleared my throat. "I was born and grew up in Hermosa Beach."

Lady smiled indulgently. "That isn't what I meant, and you know it."

I smiled back but said nothing.

"I take it that is your natural hair color," she said. "Silver and gray."

"Yes," I said.

"You don't dye it?"

"No."

"Who are your people that you have such unusual hair color?"

I knew what she was asking—was I fae or shifter or some other magical thing? I wasn't.

"My ancestors come from Western Europe, Scotland and Ireland mostly. My father was an engineer at The Aerospace Corporation. My mother was a stay-at-home mom. They were killed five years ago in a light-plane crash. My dad's best friend was the pilot."

"How very sad," Lady said, not sounding sad at all.

She looked down at her computer screen, then back up, and locked her eyes on mine. I caught the movement from the corner of my sight as she pressed a button on her desk. "Thank you for your time. Dr. Sharma will see you out."

Fine. Lady Califia could dismiss me, but not intimidate me. I returned the same eye-lock stare and added a friendly smile.

Dr. Sharma must not have been close by or he had to finish up something before he could come fetch me. We stood a long, long moment with each of us trying to establish our dominance. We stood long enough that I began to feel antsy and uncomfortable, though I never dropped my eyes from her face.

"Shall we share secrets?" she said, suddenly all best friends forever.

"If you like."

"Sit," Lady said, as affable as could be. "Please."

I sat in one of the two blue-leather chairs in front of her desk.

"When someone doesn't want to tell me something, I get very curious," she said. "I'm not one to let things go once my curiosity is aroused. I wonder why she doesn't want to tell me the answer? What in her background is so painful, shameful, or awful that she feels she must keep it caged like a rabid dog?"

"It's none of those things," I said. "I'll answer any job-related questions you like about my experience and my qualifications. I do, however, like to keep my personal and business life separate." I paused. "But if you feel like talking, I have questions for you."

Lady's eyes widened slightly, but she nodded for me to go on.

"You're very well-known," I said. "Exceptionally well-known. You're also either magical yourself or deeply involved in the magical community and yet no word of that leaks into your public persona."

A hint of smile bent her mouth. "I also like to keep my personal and professional life separate. Certain things are none of the ordinary world's business. However, if we are to work together, and that is still undecided, we must trust each other." She cocked one perfectly shaped eyebrow.

I took it as an invitation to ask away—knowing that if I did, I was going to have to respond in kind.

"Why bring us here and show us demons and sorting doors and knobs covered in runes?"

Lady regarded me. "You seem like a bright woman. You tell me why."

It didn't take much to figure out. "My supposition is either you're looking for someone who's familiar with magical worlds because whatever you need done crosses into those realms, or you've been threatened by something supernatural and need a bodyguard who isn't afraid of demons."

"Very good," she said. "You're quite near the truth, but neither guess is spot on." She leaned forward. "You do realize that anything said between us here is confidential. You'll be signing a non-disclosure agreement on the way out in any event."

"If I tell you my personal history," I said, "you'll have to sign one as well."

A single, barked laugh burst from Lady's mouth.

"You go first," she said.

I shook my head. "Not a chance."

"All right," she said. "I am," she paused for dramatic effect, "the goddess of California."

I'm not ashamed to say I sat there for a moment stunned and trying to make sense of what she'd announced and wondering if I should laugh at the joke or not. Her face and demeanor showed she was dead serious.

"Well," I said. "You've got me beat all to hell. Compared to you, I'm downright dull. And you found the treasure. And built an empire."

"Rescued the treasure," she said firmly. "I'd known it was there from the day the ship went down."

That took me aback as well.

The *Pride of Zubis* sunk off the coast of California in 1653, laden with gold, silver, and precious stones. Every schoolchild in California learned the story in the fourth grade, along with how Junipero Serra had set up the series of missions that crawled up the state. Every fourth-grader built mission replicas (I'd picked San Juan Capistrano and built it out of sugar cubes.) and made construction paper reproductions of the *Pride*. The textbooks conveniently skip over what Father Serra and the Spanish in general did to the people already living here. And whom the Spanish looted to get the precious cargo that went down with the *Pride*. It was a big deal when the *Pride* was found and salvaged by a team under the command of Lady Califia, a find that captured the imagination much the same way Robert Ballard's finding the *Titanic* had.

Lady saw the look on my face and likely reasoned that the *Pride*'s history was skipping through my mind and I was quickly doing the math.

"Well," she said, "I wasn't a goddess yet when the ship sank. One of the first things I did after I ascended was "find" that treasure. We'd lived in near poverty while I was growing up. Stupid to live hand-to-mouth when a fortune in gold and jewels is lying off your coast—coast that falls under my jurisdiction, no matter what Calypso, the sea goddess, says."

I was wondering if this highly intelligent, business-savvy woman was out of her freaking mind when she broke the short silence, saying, "I've shown you mine. Now you show me yours."

I shifted my position in the leather chair, straightening my back to get more comfortable. I didn't tell this story often. Practically never, actually.

"My people, my parents, grandparents and all, were normal and ordinary. When I was five, on a very clear day when I could see the Santa Monica Mountains like they were just down the street, I decided to go there. I let myself out of the yard and started walking."

"You were adventurous?"

"More 'acting on whatever popped into my head.'" I shrugged. "Impulsive, my mother used to say."

What she really used to say was I had no natural sense of danger and lacked all sense of caution. Mom loved me, but I exasperated her. No doubt I caused her hours of worry as well. Sad when we realize these things and it's too late to go back and say, *Sorry*.

Lady encouraged me with a tilt of her chin to continue.

I wasn't sure why it bothered me to tell this story. I'd long since come to grips with what had happened, even been glad for it. Was glad for it. Still—

"I'd gotten maybe six or seven blocks away, far outside of my usual walkabout area, when I saw something glimmering in the air in a little wooded area off the side of the road. I went to investigate. When I walked into the shimmer, I found myself not in the little copse of trees I'd seen from the road, but in a strange, heavily forested land. There were 'people' there who didn't look quite right. Some had blue, green, or bright yellow skins. Some had wings. Some had pointed ears. They all wore what looked like flowing nightgowns. They seemed very tall to me, but most everyone did then."

Telling the story, I saw it again in my mind's eye. Felt again the wonder I'd felt as a child when they'd gather around me, seeming to be as fascinated with me as I was with them. There had been a sound like a crack of thunder, though the day was clear and sunny, and a tall, beautiful woman with purple skin dressed in what I now know is chainmail strode through the throng to me. She didn't say anything, only looked me over as if taking my measure and placed her palm on my forehead. It had felt like my whole body—every bone, muscle, cell, and drop of blood—had been fast asleep and had suddenly woken. I'd started singing, of all things. The people were all laughing and clapping their hands as they pushed me out of the sparkling place and back into the wood. The next moment, I found myself back in my bedroom at home.

Lady nodded. "Touched by the spirits."

I shrugged. "When I told my mother, she looked stricken a moment and then said that couldn't have happened because

I'd been in my bedroom taking a nap for the last hour. She'd checked on me several times and knew I was there. Even after I'd looked in the mirror and seen that my hair had changed color, Mom acted as if nothing was different. When family friends or strangers would remark on the color, Mom ignored it as if she hadn't heard them."

"Your parents pretended nothing had changed?"

"My mother did, and my father mostly went along with her wishes. But he did let slip one time that it wasn't just my hair color that had changed. I had changed. Came back too sure of myself." I laughed without humor. "For a while, according to Dad, mother joked she was sure I was a changeling and not her daughter at all."

Lady's interest perked up. "Are you a changeling?"

Did a changeling know it wasn't the original? That it had been swapped?

"No. It was just her way of coping. I was too much like them to be anything other than their natural-born daughter."

Lady steepled her fingers and rested her chin on their pinnacle. "What do you think happened that day in the woods?"

I crossed my arms over my chest. "I don't know. But I was different after that. I could *feel* things. Random things like whether a rug is old or a modern reproduction. Yours is old. And I could control the elements—fire, water, air, and earth."

Lady nodded. "Yes. I saw a small demonstration of that earlier."

The first time I'd control an element, it had scared the living shit out of me. I was ten years old—long after the day the chain-mail lady had touched me—and on a field trip to the tide pools with my school class. Someone, I didn't remember exactly who anymore, said, "Wouldn't it be cool if there was a cave in the cliff?" which was behind us. "We could hide in there," my classmate had said, "and scare old Mr. Clarkston silly."

At ten, that seemed a hilarious idea. I'd focused on a spot on the hillside that I thought was where the top of the cave opening should be and sort of mentally traced out the cave's mouth in my mind. The earth began to crumble. It crumbled in exactly the shape I'd mapped out. I *knew* it was my doing without knowing how I knew or how I was doing it. I managed to make it stop, again without really understanding the *how* of things."

I tried to control different things after that—making the dog dance or people say what I wanted—stuff that seemed useful to a ten-year-old. Eventually I figured out it was the four elements that would dance to my tune. I practiced controlling them until I was as good at it as I am now.

But Lady didn't need to hear that bit of my history.

I uncrossed my arms and set my hands in my lap. "That's my story."

She tilted her head slightly. "Why you?"

That was the big question, the one that sometimes left me sleepless. Was I chosen or was it happenstance? Would anyone who'd wandered into the wood that day have had the same experience? The same change? Was there a reason to give me these particular powers or was it simply the chain-mail lady's idea of a joke? Not a very funny one if it was. Not to me.

"I don't know," I said.

Lady tapped one manicured fingernail against her desk as if thinking, and then seemed to make up her mind about something.

"Congratulations," she said. "You've won the position.

You start tomorrow, nine o'clock sharp. I don't tolerate lateness."

I cleared my throat. "What, exactly, does the job entail?"

She smiled and leaned across the desk toward to me. "Hunting. You're going to love it."

Hunting was a broad mandate.

Before I could ask, *Hunting what?* Lady pulled a Montblanc pen—a much more expensive version of the ones we'd used to write our 'eyewitness reports'—and a piece of what looked like thick, expensive writing paper from a desk drawer.

"What's your name?" she asked as she wrote something on the paper.

"Shayna Greene," I said. "Shay."

"Well, Shayna," she said, handing me the paper with an address now written on it, "I believe we will have a fruitful collaboration."

4

The 405 freeway was jammed as usual. The paper with the address on it lay folded in my purse, like a ticking time bomb.

There were a myriad of weird things in the world that most people were unaware of, and I'd seen my share of them, but a goddess? The goddess of California? That was a bit farfetched even for me—and I was someone with silver-gray hair and superpowers granted by whatever it was I'd run into in the wood. I'd worked for wizards, witches, and once for a werewolf. I knew there was more to the world than what most people saw. But gods and goddesses? That was the stuff of old mythologies.

As soon as I'd reached the parking lot and climbed into my car, I'd googled *Califia*. Not Lady Califia, which would give me gazillions of articles about the woman I'd just left, but Califia alone—an unusual last name—to maybe learn something about her people and background.

Calafia or Califia, it turned out, was the name of a fictional warrior queen who ruled over a kingdom of women living on the Island of California. A Spanish writer, Garcia Rodriguez de Montalvo, had invented her for a novel written around 1500. The state was named for the fictional queen. In the stop and go freeway traffic, I turned the information over in my mind and wondered, *What did that say about Lady?*

That she'd developed her persona and taken that name for reasons known only to her?

That she was mad as a hatter?

Or, and this was the hardest to wrap my head around, she really was the goddess of California.

Why would a goddess need to hire someone like me? My specialty was rescue and recovery, not hunting—whatever that meant to her. Though maybe it was just semantics. I hunted for the person or thing that had been taken, and then brought he, she, or it back. But the word *hunting* usually meant something else. Find and capture. Or find and kill.

Hunting what? I wondered again.

I wondered if I truly wanted this job. *Hunting* of the capture or kill variety wasn't my thing. Neither was working for someone who made up a name and history so farfetched as to be laughable. How could I trust anything she said to be true? And if she was crazy as well as magical—that opened up lots of unpleasant possible consequences for anyone in her employ.

My conclusion was that I really *didn't* want the job.

I pulled off the freeway on Rosecrans Avenue, heading for home, the decision reached that I'd call Lady in the morning and tell her to find another *companion*.

For the last seven years I've rented the small back house of a two-on-a-lot in North Hermosa Beach. Darci and Bella, my landladies who lived in the big front house, were great. I counted them among my friends, and not only because they'd raised my rent only once in all that time.

When I pulled onto my block, I saw several big trucks parked in front of my address. I sped forward, worried about Darci and Bella. I pulled into the long driveway that led to my house but couldn't get close to my front door. A big van painted Dutch yellow and sporting *Water Damage Specialists* written on its side blocked the long driveway. A thick blue hose leading from the van ran across the drive and into my house through a window.

Darci stood in my doorway, wringing her hands. She turned and hurried toward me when she saw my car pull up.

I got out and walked toward her saying, "What happened?"

My landlady ran a hand through her short hair, cut man-style, and dyed a vibrant pink with blue tips.

"I don't know. About an hour after you left this morning, I started smelling something bad. I traced it to your house. I used my key and let myself in." Her face crumpled. "It's a world-class mess in there, Shay. The damage specialist guys say the street sewer backed up into your house at about the same time that the major water pipes to your house broke."

Stunned, I stuttered, "How-how can that happen?"

Darci shook her head. "I don't know. The damage guys say they've never seen it happen before. Not two things at once like that. One guy said maybe the sewer backing up put too much pressure on the pipes, the pipes going from the street to the house are old, and the pressure made them burst inside your house."

"Oh, my God," I muttered and stepped past her to look in the front door. A man wearing yellow rubber waders and a filter mask was on his pad-covered knees with the business end of the thick blue hose, siphoning water from the floor. All the windows had been opened and several big fans were blowing air around the room. I sniffed and wrinkled my nose. The room smelled of shit and garbage. The water level had gotten at least a couple of feet high, I saw by the soaked remnant of my living room couch, and spray must have gone higher, since the walls were wet almost to the ceiling. Soggy books floated in the few inches of water still remaining. One of my dining chairs was turned over, its back submerged. My heart sank. Tears welled in my eyes for my ruined things. I wiped them away and turned to Darci.

"Your homeowners insurance covers this, right?"

She gave me a tightlipped nod. "The structural damage, but not for your stuff." She paused and looked hopeful. "Do you have renter's insurance?"

I didn't.

I called out to Mr. Damage Specialist over the whir of the industrial strength fans and the gulp and gurgle of the sucking hose. "What do the bedroom, kitchen, and the bath look like?"

The workman looked up at me and shook his head. "About like this," he called back through his filter mask.

Tears threatened in my eyes again, but I blinked them away. Much of what I owned was ruined, or nearly so. I had money in the bank, but not enough money to completely refurnish my house, not even at Goodwill. Much of my clothes and definitely my shoes on the floor of the closet would be ruined. I thanked my lucky stars that my photo albums were in a dresser drawer and my weapons were locked in my garage. But many more of my books were probably wrecked. I had keepsakes on my bookshelves in the bedroom as well, things that couldn't be replaced if they were waterlogged.

"Jesus," I muttered, the implications pinging through my brain. "Where am I going to sleep tonight?"

Darci touched my arm. "You can stay with us until the house is dry and safe to move back into."

It was a kind and generous offer, but I didn't think I could stand company tonight. Besides, I'd sat on their lovely but somewhat lumpy couch hundreds of times and knew I wouldn't like sleeping on it.

"A friend of mine manages a residence hotel in Torrance," I said. "I think I'll see if he has a room open."

At least packing would be easy, as all the clothes I currently had access to were on my back. I didn't much feel like trucking through the muck to rescue any clothes that might have been above the waterline or escaped the spray. There was time for that later.

"When can I get in to assess things?" I called again to the man.

"We'll have the standing water out of here in a few hours," he called back. "It'll be days before everything is completely dry."

Lovely.

I stood a few more silent moments, but really, there was nothing I could do here. I made my farewells to Darci, got back in my car, and called my friend. He had a room I could have.

I'm not someone who much liked shopping to begin with, but shopping in the face of disaster was doubly daunting. On my way to the residence hotel, I stopped at J.C. Penny and picked up underwear and socks, a few shirts, and a pair of pajamas. I stopped at a CVS and bought a toothbrush, toothpaste, and a hairbrush.

Lying on my back in the hotel room, some movie I wasn't paying attention to playing on the TV with the sound turned way down, I counted my blessings. I still had my car, my phone, and my credit cards. I had some money in the bank. And I had a job I didn't really want with Lady Califia.

5

The address Lady had written down was on the hill in Palos Verdes. Way up high on the hill. High enough that when the fog rolled in, my bet was that it would completely surround the house, hiding it from view.

Not today, though. Today the morning sun shone like a beacon, its amber rays picking out the sprawling one-story house at the end of a private road in a bright light while the land around it lay in shadow. This wasn't a normal weather phenomenon, but I was beginning to understand that normal wasn't a word used in conjunction with Lady Califia.

The house itself was Craftsman style, with brown shake shingles covering the exterior walls and a wide, red brick porch leading to the front door. Some of the bricks had an image impressed into it. I spotted dragonfly, hummingbird, grasshopper, horned lizard, and snake. My bet was they were all native to the state.

The large house spread over the lot like a lazy cat stretching in the warmth. The front door, I saw as I walked up the brick steps, was a double. A rearing bear was carved on one door, and an eagle in flight, its talons outstretched, on the other. The skill of the carver and the beauty of the detail made the doors both intimidating and welcoming at the same time. I had the distinct feeling that no matter what happened in the outside world, anyone ensconced behind the bear and eagle would be safe.

I knocked on the door. A tall, frankly gorgeous-looking, and rather muscular man in his late thirties, I guessed, almost immediately answered my knock. He wore blue jeans, a blue and white checked button up shirt with short sleeves, and brown-leather work boots. His wavy brown hair was worn collar length. His eyes were a dark, velvety hazel.

"Come in, Ms. Greene," he said, pulling the bear-side door open wide. "Lady is waiting for you on the back veranda."

Veranda! Now there was a word you didn't hear every day.

Mr. Beefy led me down a long, long hallway toward the back of the house. Closed doors broke up the expanse of hallway and I wondered what was behind them. More California landscapes hung on the walls.

At the end of the hall was another door, this one with glass in the top half. Etched into the glass was a drawing of the *Pride of Zubris* as she must have looked under sail. Through the glass, I saw Lady Califia. She wore a lemon-colored sundress with cornflower blue dots, or maybe some kind of small print, I couldn't tell from here. She was sitting on a white wicker patio chair with a green and yellow flora patterned cushion. An identical chair was near her, with a small, round wrought iron table in between. Past her, a garden of flowers, vegetables, and herbs took up what probably would be lawn in other homes around here—maybe with a croquet course set up on it. It was barely April, but every plant was in bloom or bearing fruit. Bees hummed happily and butterflies fluttered around like we'd dropped into some Disney movie. The air was sweet with the scent of roses, orange blossoms and honeysuckle. A pond as large as an Olympic swimming pool lay off to the left. A pair of ducks with maybe half a dozen ducklings swam lazily on its surface.

Mr. Beefy opened the door and stepped aside for me to go onto the *veranda*. I smiled slightly, enjoying the sound of that word in my head. *Veranda*. It fit both the house and Lady Califia.

Lady gestured toward the empty chair for me to sit. I did and took in the view to the north and west. We were too high up and far away to see the waves crashing against the rocky shore. From here the ocean seemed to be a wide stretch of green blue that bumped up against the brighter blue of the sky. I could get used to a view like this.

Mr. Beefy came out and laid a tray with a deco-style teapot—blue with gold embellishments—and two teacups on the little table between the chairs. There was also a matching sugar bowl, a tiny pitcher of cream, a dish of lemon wedges, and a large white plate piled high with strawberry scones that didn't look store-bought.

"Tea?" Lady said.

"Thank you," I said and watched as she poured tea into first my cup and then into hers. She managed to make the movements as graceful and stylish as ballet. Maybe when you were a goddess that sort of grace came naturally. I laughed inside myself at the thought.

"Sugar? Cream? Lemon?" she asked.

"Plain," I said.

Lady smiled. "Help yourself to the scones. Have you eaten breakfast?"

"Some," I said. I'd stopped at a McDonald's and had a not very tasty egg mcmuffin.

I picked up a scone and bit into it. It was heavenly. The tea was green. It smelled and tasted faintly of jasmine. I liked it a lot.

Lady took her tea with sugar and lemon. She stirred the tea idly, as if her mind were far away.

I ate my scone and wondered if it would be rude if I tucked the rest of them in my purse for later. Yeah. Probably.

"I like my employees to be happy," she said, suddenly back from wherever her thoughts had wandered. "Are you happy, Shayna?"

It was an odd question, but I hid my surprise. "In general, yes."

She raised her eyebrows slightly. "So you are not accepting this job out of desperation?"

I considered my possible replies and went for honesty. If Lady were a goddess, maybe she had access to some sort of Akashic Records or something, had checked up on me, and would know if I were lying. But I didn't have to be specific about why I needed the money more today than yesterday.

"I had some reservations, but I've decided to take the job."

Lady sipped her tea and set her cup down. "And are committed to it."

"Yes, unless you ask me to do something immoral. I have my standards."

"And what if I asked you to do something illegal?"

"It would depend on what it was," I said, lifting my teacup. "When you do rescue and recovery, sometimes a thing might not be quite legal, but it is moral and right and therefore okay in my book."

"And if you had to hurt someone?"

"It would depend on who and why." I took a sip of tea

and set the cup down. "I'm not a thug. I try not to hurt people or get hurt myself."

Lady smiled. "Good."

"But I would like to know more about this job I've accepted."

"The duties are varied," Lady said. "For your first assignment, I want you to find and recover an aubergine pearl necklace that was stolen from the sea goddess, Calypso. Not that Calypso is her real name any more than Lady Califia is mine, but Calypso will do for conversation between us."

I filed that away, not knowing if the issue of names was important or not. But recovery of stolen property—that was right in my wheelhouse.

"Do you have any idea where it might be?" I asked.

Lady picked up her teacup and held it in the air in front of her. "A suitor of mine, Michael Rawlings is his name, stole it from Calypso to make it a gift to me. It's true I'd expressed admiration for the quality of the pearls, but I never meant for him to steal them." She paused. "Calypso and I have history. I told you yesterday that she considered the *Pride of Zubis* to belong to her since it was sunk in her domain. But its cargo had been stolen from the land, and was therefore mine to claim."

I shrugged that off. Disputes between goddesses were their business. Mine was to recover whatever my employer sent me after.

"Is it just a matter of asking Michael Rawlings to give it back?"

"If only it were that simple," Lady said and sighed. "Michael has disappeared. His gift of the pearls was not enough for me to accept him as a potential lover—silly boy. When I turned him down—politely, mind you, but firmly—he stomped off with the necklace like a child and then seemingly fell off the earth. He certainly isn't in California or I'd feel him, unless he was under a hiding spell or a curse—which is possible. I've spoken with my sisters—Oregon, Washington, and Colorado—and he's not there. My brother, Arizona, has some bug up his nose and won't speak to me. Let's say that as far as I can ascertain, he's not in the western states. Which is not to say he took the necklace with him wherever he went. It could be in a safe deposit box in Long Beach for all I know."

"So, you have nothing for me to go on?"

"A deadline," Lady said. "Calypso has sworn to flood me as far inland as the San Andreas Fault if her necklace isn't returned by Saturday. With ocean water. Salt. Which will ruin the land."

My eyes widened. "Can she do that?"

"Oh, yes. And I've no doubt she will. She can be quite vengeful. So, time is of the essence."

I fiddled with my teacup. "Saturday is only four days off. With nothing to go on— Where would I start?"

"You might want to speak with Michael's sister, Miranda. I'll give you her address. She won't speak to me, witch that she is, but she might to talk you. Especially if you had an enticing story. Perhaps he's come into a bit of money and you've been hired to find him."

I'd caught something in Lady's statement. "Did you say bitch or witch?"

Lady smiled thinly. "Most definitely a capital W Witch. Powerful. And a bitch, too."

I was quiet a moment, thoughts racing in my head.

"I went by your house last night," Lady said, startling me.

"Why?"

"I like to see where my employees live. A person's home says much about them. You seem to have had a bit of trouble."

"Some flooding. It should be fine in a week." I said it casually, but the idea that she'd gone to my house annoyed me. Off the clock is off the clock and privacy isn't something an employer has the right to invade. There was something weird and almost creepy about it.

Lady put down the cup she'd been holding and leaned toward me. "You must stay here, then, in the meantime. I won't have you sleeping on friends' couches or spending good money on bad motel rooms. I want you well-rested and as worry-free as possible when you come to work each morning."

I didn't like her assumption that I should jump at the chance to be under her roof. I lived alone for a reason. I liked my privacy and the freedom to come and go as I pleased without having to worry about someone else.

"I have a place to stay. Thank you for the offer, though."

She peered at me. "I insist."

A rush of lightheadedness swept through me, and I really, really wanted to accept her offer. Who wouldn't want to stay in this beautiful house? I felt grateful that she'd be so kind.

I pulled my hands into fists and held my breath until the feeling passed.

"You have power," I said.

Lady lifted one shoulder in a shrug. "I don't do magic tricks. That's why I have you. But I do have certain capabilities."

"Hmmm," I noised, not happy with having an employer who thought she could control me. Who, in fact, very nearly had. "I think it's healthy to have some. . . physical distance. . . between the work and home space."

Lady regarded me. "There are advantages to you for staying here. Expense, for one."

I did the math in my head—the cost of the hotel room vs.

free at Lady's. The cost of a hotel room deducted from the money available to buy all the things I'd need to replace.

She pursed her lips. "Shayna, it makes sense for you stay here. Agree, and I will give my word to not try to influence or compel you from the moment you say yes onward."

I wondered why it seemed so important to her and said so.

"Because time is short and I want you available for whatever I need, whenever I need it."

I sat very still. I didn't like ultimatums and I really didn't like employers who thought their fee bought all of my time for whatever purpose they wanted.

"Saturday, Shayna," Lady said. "Calypso must have the pearls in her hand by then or my land will be ruined. If that happens, your little house will be under much more water than it is now. Saltwater. Your home. Your friends' homes and businesses. Your lovely town—it all will be ruined. Our beloved California will be devastated—unless we find and return those pearls. I need you here, available on short notice should there be cause."

Put like that—

"If I have your word you won't try to influence or compel me to do anything from this moment on," I said, "I'll stay."

Lady inclined her head. "You have it."

I believed her. If there was one thing that stood out in my reading about Lady Califia it was her strict adherence to keeping her promises.

"Now," Lady said, "let's discuss some other avenues you may want to explore to find the necklace."

A thought struck me. I held up one finger in a *wait* sign. "Why don't you talk to Miranda yourself? You said she won't talk to you, but I've felt your persuasive power. Witch or not, you could get her to tell you what you want to know."

Lady shot me an indulgent smile. "I am a goddess,

Shayna, and I am Lady Califia. A brilliant businesswoman does not knock on someone's door demanding information on an erstwhile lover, much less use her powers on said mortal who would be only too quick to tell the world about it. Not if she expects to retain respect from the human business and the godly communities."

I could see her point.

6

Michael's witchy sister lived in the north end of Redondo Beach, which was less beach town and more typical Los Angeles suburb with single-family homes built in the 50s, and a smattering of big property-line-to-property-line new homes for the aspirational.

The witch, whose given name was Miranda, seemed to be doing well, to judge by where she lived. The faux Victorian painted white with blue trim on the windows and gingerbread stood out as a bit of old-time elegance in the block of stucco-walled mini mansions. It was foolish to think kindly toward a person simply because you liked their taste in architecture, but I found myself hoping she'd be open and easy to talk to, that I'd get the information I needed, compliment her on her house, and be on my way.

Miranda opened the door at my knock. I assumed it was her from the description Lady had given me: medium height, blue-black hair hanging to her waist, startling blue eyes. She wore a long, flowing teal tunic over a long flowing darker teal skirt, and cinnamon-colored, fabric ankle boots with flowers embroidered on the toes. Very boho.

"Yes?" she said politely. "Can I help you?"

Before I could speak, she sniffed once and her face hardened. It was pretty clear she'd caught a whiff of my magic. I smiled apologetically and shrugged one shoulder.

"Lady Califia sent me," I said, since straightforward seemed the best tactic now. "I wondered if you might know and be willing to tell me where your brother, Michael, is. I need to speak to him."

Her face screwed up and she started to slam the door in my face.

Well, that was rude.

I summoned up a bit of wind to help me push the door open and stepped inside the house, straight into her living room.

"You know who I am," Miranda said between clenched teeth. "What I am. I will demonstrate my powers for you if you do not turn around and leave my home this second."

I gave her a placating smile. "I only know that you are sister to the man Lady Califia believes stole a pearl necklace. All I want to do is talk to him."

"Ha!" she barked. "I dearly doubt that 'talk' is what you have in mind. Not if that prime bitch, Califia, sent you."

I kept the placating smile plastered on my face and turned my hands palms outward in sign that I meant her no harm. "I've been hired to locate and return the necklace to its rightful owner. If your brother has it and gives it to me, no harm will come to him."

Miranda drew her arms into her sides and clenched her fists. I was pretty sure she was readying a spell, but I didn't want to attack her if she wasn't. Magical pissing matches were way down on my list of fun times and how to get things done. I much prefer simple conversation.

Evidently Miranda preferred her method. I felt her

revving up the spell before she started the incantation. I try to give people the chance to change their mind and stand down, so I waited until she was almost committed to throwing her magic before I readied fire.

The spell hurtled toward me faster than I'd expected. I'd barely gotten a firewall up—which would look to her more like a heat mirage than what it truly was—before her spell hit. Her magic sparked and sizzled as it burned away.

Miranda laughed. Which was not the reaction I'd expected.

"Okay then," she said, a bright gleam lighting her eyes. "Game on."

I kept my voice placid. "It would be easier for both of us if you'd tell me where your brother is. Tell me, and I'll be on my way."

I felt her begin to ready another spell. Miranda wasn't stupid. The next spell would almost certainly have an anti-fire component to it, maybe an anti-air one as well if she'd realized I'd used air to force her front door open. I can control the four elements—fire, water, earth, and wind—but a smart opponent will figure that out after watching my strikes and counterstrikes for a while. Once my opponent guards against all four elements, I'm pretty much shit out of luck. Not that I'm a one-trick pony. I can do loads of interesting combinations and expressions with my four elements. But I seriously was not in the mood for a fight today.

You know that scene in one of the Indiana Jones movies where Indy is facing off with the swordsman who's doing all these fancy things with his scimitar and Indy just takes out his gun and shoots him? That was pretty much how I felt. Just get it done; fuck all the fancy spellwork shit.

I set loose up a minor earthquake, confined to the footprint of Miranda's house. The floor bucked and rolled. Unprepared, Miranda stumbled. She put out her hand to use my shoulder to catch her balance. I twisted away. Miranda stutter-stepped another couple of paces and fell to one knee.

"Bitch!" she screamed as she tried to climb back up to her feet.

I sighed and sent another bout of the ground beneath her house shaking. She tumbled onto her back. I put my foot on her chest, holding her down.

She grabbed my leg around the calf and tried to pull me down with her. I summoned up a cocoon of air around me to keep me upright and a layer to keep her held down.

I kept the ground beneath us shaking. Photographs in frames and small pieces of pottery on a shelf rattled against each other. A mirror on the wall swung like a pendulum. I saw the look change in her eyes as she realized she couldn't get up and that pretty quick all her bric-a-brac on shelves and books in her bookcase were going to start falling.

It seemed stupid to make her wait. I sent another shockwave under the foundation. Pottery danced to the edge of the shelf and crashed onto the hardwood floor. The large mirror followed, broken glass sliding across the room. The big flat screen TV on another wall began shimmying.

"All right," she spat. "Stop. You win."

I slightly lifted my foot on her chest. "You swear on your honor and the honor of all who came before you that you will not try to harm me if I let you go?"

She gritted her teeth, but said, "I swear."

I stopped the earthquake and took my foot off her chest. She sat up and stared around her living room.

"Look what you've done!" she wailed. "What was the point?"

I'd have thought the point was obvious. "All I want is

some information. Tell me what I need to know, and I'll be on my way."

She gritted her teeth a moment and then blew out a harsh breath that seemed to calm her. "At least the couch is still in place. You want to sit?"

I nodded and followed her to a long couch, maybe eight feet, covered in red brocade. She sat at one end and I sat at the other. The cushions were comfortable and the back supportive. Except for the red brocade, I wouldn't have minded having this in my own home.

We sat in silence, staring at each other. Taking each other's measure, I thought. At least that's what I was doing. I judged that I'd made my point with her and she wouldn't try to bullshit me now. Miranda, I thought, was the type that talked tough but folded when challenged.

"Do you know where your brother is?" I said.

She started to sneer, then caught herself and banished the urge. "As it happens, I don't. I haven't heard from him since," she looked up at the ceiling as if the date were written there, "winter solstice."

I tsked. "You could have told me that in the first place."

She shrugged. "I could have. But since Lady Califia sent you, I assumed a fight would come sooner or later. I went for sooner."

I filed that away, too. Did Lady usually send people to do her bidding who fought first and asked questions later? If so, she was going to be disappointed in me as an employee.

"Did your brother steal a pearl necklace?"

Miranda sighed. "Yes. He showed it to me. I told him that messing with Calypso was a fool's game, but he was smitten with Lady Califia and thought his show of daring would sway her to his side. Maybe even make her love him."

Her face grew dark. "You know she does that—makes

men fall in love with her for amusement. She's a fucking bitch."

I smiled thinly. "She says the same about you."

"Good," Miranda said. "She makes a better enemy than friend. Something you might keep in mind."

"We're not friends or enemies," I said. "I work for her, that's all."

Miranda leaned toward me. "With humans, even magical humans like us, we make a certain kind of sense to each other. But the gods and goddesses, they're capricious and crazy. They live a long, long time and they get bored. Toying with humans makes a pleasant diversion for them. You might want to find other employment."

So, Miranda knew Lady was a goddess. She probably knew Calypso was as well. Did most people in the magical community here know about their existence, or did Miranda know a mostly well-kept secret? Lady's announcement of her godhood had been a surprise to me.

I really needed to get out more.

I cleared my throat. "If you had to guess where your brother was, where would that be?"

She shook her head. "We were never that close."

"No favorite place he liked to go. No friend he might turn to?"

Miranda sighed and closed her eyes a moment. "Michael had a girlfriend for a while. Maybe still, for all I know. A Japanese girl named Kimiko. I've been to her place. I think I can find the address for you."

She got up and disappeared into another room. I looked around the living room. It was going to be a bit of a mess to clean up. I didn't feel bad about the things that had broken. Just annoyed Miranda had made it necessary.

She returned with a piece of paper in her hand that she gave to me. I glanced at the address.

"Take it and go," she said, forgetting that she'd been polite a couple of minutes earlier. "And don't come back."

I stood and smiled. "Not unless I have to, and I hope I don't."

The residence hotel where I had a room was only a little out of my way between Miranda's and the girlfriend. I headed back to the hotel for a quick freshen up.

In my room with a lovely view of the parking lot, I showered, refreshed my lipstick, and wrapped my hair up into a bun—to keep it out of my way in case the girlfriend also wanted to fight. Having it up in a bun instead of flowing down my back also helped people not get distracted by its color. Sometimes that distraction served me, but I had the feeling that the fewer distractions with the girlfriend the better. I wanted her focused on one thing only—telling me where Michael was. If I were lucky, he'd be with her.

I packed my meager belongings back in the J.C. Penny and CVS bags I'd carried them here in. I still wasn't crazy about the idea of staying at Lady's mansion on the hill, but it was free and given the short time frame to recover the necklace, it made sense.

I grabbed the room key and headed downstairs to check out. Unfortunately, my friend wasn't on duty. Fortunately, he'd adjusted the room rate in the computer for me. I put the fare on my credit card and made a mental note to ask Lady when payday was.

7

Last year had been a good one for me financially and I'd made a modest pile of money. I'd spent a good portion of it on a new car, a silver Honda Clarity, which at the moment was low on both battery for the electric motor and on gas. I swung into a station on Prairie Avenue on my way to Gardena to talk to Kimiko, the girlfriend. The fight with the sister/witch had dried my throat. Fortunately, the gas station had a little convenience store attached to it and I went inside to buy a bottle of water. It irked me to pay two dollars plus tax for a bottle of water I could buy at the grocery store for sixty-seven cents, but thirst will make me spend my money now rather than fifteen minutes later when I could find a regular market.

I opened my wallet and saw no green paper at all and only three quarters and four pennies in the change pocket. No problem. That's why I carry a credit card, right? I was pulling out my card when a male voice behind me said, "Allow me." A hand shot forward and put two dollars and change on the counter by the cash register.

We're a friendly, helpful bunch here in the South Bay. It's

not unusual for a stranger to pony up if someone is short on cash for a small purchase. I turned to thank my benefactor. He was tall, thin, and nice looking, with the muscles and build of a dedicated runner. His brown eyes sparkled, betraying the intelligence of his mind, and his smile was wide and infectious.

"Thank you," I said.

"My pleasure," he said with a nod, and stepped up to put his purchases—a bag of chips and a larger bottle of water than I'd bought—on the counter.

I walked out smiling, happy over the brief encounter and bit of unexpected kindness that came with no expectations.

I got into my now fully gassed-up car, popped the lid on the bottled water and took a deep swallow, then headed for Gardena. I'd programmed the address into my phone earlier. It didn't take long for the disembodied directions voice to say, "Arrived. Your destination is on the right."

The girlfriend's apartment complex looked like a lot of apartment buildings in the area—two stories, yellow stucco walls, brown trim on the windows and fascia board, with black, wrought iron fencing around the grounds. Thankfully the gate didn't need a code to open and was unlocked. I found a parking spot out front and went through the gate. I stood a moment to oriented myself, figured out how the apartment numbering went, and found her door.

There was no answer to my repeated knock.

"She's probably at work," a voice behind me said.

I turned to see a middle-aged man dressed all in tan with grass stains on the knees of his pants and a trowel in his right hand.

I smiled and tried to look like I might be an acquaintance of Kimiko's. "Do you know where she works?"

He shook his head. "No idea, but a lot of times she wears scrubs when she leaves in the morning."

Doctors, nurses, and physician's assistants in hospitals and in private practice wore scrubs. So did dental hygienists and students studying to be everything from medical assistants to chiropractors. I'd even been in a foot massage place once where the workers wore scrubs. Kimiko's attire was less than useless in trying to ferret out where she worked.

"Okay. Thanks," I said and started walking back toward the street.

I stopped and turned back to the gardener. "Does a man —" I fumbled inside my purse for the photo of Michael that Lady had given me, found it and pulled it out. "Have you seen this man around? Visiting Kimiko?"

The gardener looked at it and shook his head. "Not for a while, I think. He could have come around when I wasn't here."

I was about to thank him for his help when he reached out and touched my arm. He glanced over my head and dropped his voice low. "That's her."

I turned and put a wide smile on my face.

"Kimiko," I called, making my voice sound like I knew her and giving a little wave.

She turned, an expectant look on her face until she realized she didn't know me. I walked up to her.

"Hi. I'm Shay Greene. I'm looking for Michael Rawlings."

Blunt and straightforward can have its uses. It could often make people answer before they thought too carefully.

I might as well have said I was the devil come to claim her soul, that's how fast she turned and ran toward her apartment. I followed at a walk. I must have really spooked her because she was fumbling with her key at the door, unable to fit it into the slot.

I reached out and gently took the keys from her hand. "Here, let me help."

Kimiko's eyes were wide with fear. The moment the door was unlocked, she shoved it open, jammed inside, and tried to slam the door shut in my face.

I sighed. Two slammed-in-my-face doors in one day. I could start feeling like it was personal.

I leaned forward putting my shoulder against the door and pushing so she couldn't shut it all the way.

"You don't have to invite me in," I said into the slim crack between the door and the jambs. "Just come outside where—" I turned slightly and gestured at the gardener and then at a mom and her two kids splashing in the building's pool. "—you have witnesses. Come outside and talk to me for a minute. I promise it won't take long."

Kimiko warily stepped back outside. "What do you want?"

"As I said, I'm trying to find Michael Rawlings. Do you have any idea where he is?"

Kimiko spat on the little patch of grass next to the concrete in front of her door. "That cheatin' bastard. No. I don't. And I don't want to."

"Cheating?"

Kimiko's head jiggled like a bobble-head dog in a car on a rough road. "He comes to my house one night. Takes off his coat, gets comfortable, like always. When he gets up to take a leak, I notice a small white box in his coat pocket. Well, you can't blame a girl for looking. Inside was a pearl necklace! I know pearls. I come from a line of pearl divers. These were aubergine, perfectly matched, and very, very valuable. I'm thinking they're a gift for me. Michael knows I love and value pearls. He comes back out, sees me looking at them, grabs me around the throat and says, 'Put that down.'"

"Yikes," I said sympathetically. "He doesn't seem like a very good boyfriend."

Kimiko shifted from foot to foot. "Up until that moment, I thought he was. He'd never laid a hand on me. Treated me with respect. But he got this wild look in his eyes when he saw me with the pearls. I dropped the necklace right onto the couch. He snatched it up, shoved it in his coat pocket and was out the door faster than you could say 'mermaid's tears.' Mermaid's tears, that's what some people call pearls. Anyway. That was the last time I saw him. I phoned him the next day, but his phone was disconnected."

I kept the sympathetic look on my face as I reached into my purse and pulled out one of my cards. "If you happen to see or hear from him, would you let me know?"

She took the card and tucked it into her pocket. "Sure, if you promise something terrible will happen to him when you get a hold of the bastard."

I smiled. "I can't promise, but I think my boss is pretty unhappy with him and she's not a nice person."

Kimiko tapped the pocket where she'd stowed the card. "Good. I'll definitely call you."

I walked back to my car thinking it takes all kinds to make up a world.

Including, evidently, the man who'd paid for my water at the gas station. He was leaning against a black Ford Explorer and looking down at his phone when I stepped back on the sidewalk in front of the apartments.

I stopped in front of him. "Are you following me?"

He looked up from his phone and nodded.

Stalkers creep me out. I readied air to knock him back if he lunged for me or tried to touch me in any way. I was glad

I'd be going back to Lady's house on the hill from here and not to my house.

"Well," he said, flashing that wide, innocent-seeming grin, "not actually following. By coincidence we were coming to the same place."

"Uh huh," I said, my voice laden with sarcasm. I shifted to the left and walked past him.

"Did Kimiko Sakai have anything interesting to say?" he called after me.

I turned back and stared at him. "Excuse me?"

"Michael Rawling's girlfriend. One of them at least. Seems he was quite the player."

I stopped and turned to face him. "And you were coming to see her why?"

He shrugged. "We have the same boss and are looking for the same thing."

That took me aback.

"Ms. Califia is big on redundancy," he said.

I'd check on the truth of that when I got back to the house on the hill.

He eyed me up and down. "I take it you're the 'last ditch effort?'"

I half coughed/half laughed. "The what?"

"I've been on this case for a couple of weeks now. The boss is getting nervous, with the deadline coming up. I knew she was interviewing. You're the new face, so—"

Did competition make him angry? More determined to be the one to find the necklace? Did it matter who found it since we—I assumed it was the same for both of us—were on salary?

"Michael had more than one girlfriend?" I asked, changing the subject.

The man nodded.

"Have you spoken to all of them? All except Kimiko, I mean."

"Some."

"And?"

"And I'm not sharing information," he said. "There's a hefty bonus for whoever returns the necklace."

Except that he'd just shared two pieces of information: that there was more than one hunter looking for the necklace, and that Lady Califia had offered him a bonus for being the finder but hadn't offered one to me. She and I would have words about that.

"Good luck to you. Even with two of us hunting, my chances are at least fifty percent of finding it first." I paused as if a thought had only just suddenly struck me. "If we shared information, that percentage could go to one hundred for both of us."

He barked a laugh. "It's pretty obvious you're new. Redundancy for Ms. Califia doesn't mean one and a back-up. There are five looking for the necklace that I know of, though two are partners, so four. There could even be more."

The number took me aback. Why did Lady go through that elaborate dance to hire me if she already had people trying to retrieve the necklace? Did she really think I brought something extra to the table, or was it just a matter of throwing bodies at the problem until someone solved it?

But then, my specialty was rescue and recovery, not simply discovery of the pearls' location. It was one thing to know where something was, another to secure and return it.

"Still five," I said. "The partners may have to share the bonus, but they have twice the brains and eyes of those working alone. If I don't find it first, my money is on them to bring in the prize."

"Because they are two," he said.

"Exactly."

He leaned back against the car and regarded me. "You're suggesting we should partner as well."

I shook my head. "I work alone. I'm suggesting we share information to save us both time and," I paused, "redundancy. If you discover where the necklace is, you're welcome to the bonus. My job is to recover the thing and bring it to Lady. The hunt is merely prelude."

"The dangerous part."

"Sometimes," I said.

He crossed his arms over his chest. "What if I find and return the necklace?"

"Then you will have done the dangerous as well as the tedious part."

He laughed, uncrossed his arms, and held out his hand. "Drew Miller. Do you like *pho*? There's a great little place not far from here."

I'd heard of him. The magic community wasn't so large that you wouldn't hear about others who did work similar to yours, but we hadn't met. I clasped his hand and shook it. "Shay Greene, and I do, as a matter of fact."

His eyebrows rose slightly, which I took to mean that he'd heard of me, too.

I followed him to a little hole-in-the-wall called *Pho Eva in Your Heart*. He waited while I finished parking my car and when we walked up to the restaurant together, he held the door for me. I do appreciate a gentleman, even if he's a rival.

It was a 'seat yourself' place. We picked a table and a college-aged waiter who I guessed to be Vietnamese trotted right over to take our order. I chose vegetarian *pho chay*. Drew opted for *chow chow* soup.

"Tit for tat," he said after the waiter had gone. "You tell me what you've learned, and I'll tell you what I've learned."

He'd worked for Lady before and would know the ins and outs of her habits and peculiarities—which all employers had—better than I would. And he was eyeing a big, fat bonus if he came in with the goods.

"You first," I said.

He flashed a grin. "You don't trust me?"

I hiked one shoulder in a shrug that gave my answer.

"Okay," he said. "Michael Rawlings took the item two and a half weeks ago. He was seen making off with it, so there's no doubt of his guilt. The item's owner chased him herself, or rather her agents did, and saw him go to Lady Califia's house." He grinned. "Have you been there? It's spectacular. Amazing view."

I nodded, the barest acknowledgement. I didn't want him distracting me with a tangent and then giving me no more information than I already knew.

"Ms. Califia didn't see him that day," Drew continued. "Edwin—have you met Edwin?"

"The big guy who lives there?"

Drew nodded. "Edwin said Michael came up to the door but then slunk around to the side of the house. I suspect he knew Calypso's agents were on his tail and he wanted to throw them off, make them think he'd gone in the house. He'd be protected there. None of Calypso's agents would dare invade Ms. Califia's sanctum."

Our meals arrived and we put off talking long enough to sample the fare. The *pho* was delicious. After three or four bites, I wanted Drew to get back on track.

"So, Michael never went into the house?"

Drew shook his head. "Like I said, slunk around the side, according to Edwin, and then, after a while, just left."

"Edwin didn't find that odd or unusual?"

"He probably did, but he's not one to invite people in when the boss isn't there."

"Or go outside and question Michael?"

Drew shrugged. "You have to ask him about that. He says he didn't. He says he was more interested in and concerned about Calypso's henchmen who never came on to the property but did hang around out front for a while."

This was all vaguely interesting, but it wasn't getting me any closer to retrieving the necklace.

"What led you to Kimiko Sakai's apartment today?" I asked.

Drew put down his spoon. "I've been visiting his girlfriends one by one. Kimiko was next on the list."

"How did you know about these women?"

"Lady gave me a list. She'd had Michael thoroughly checked out when he started trying to court her. They'd met at some charity function. He's a trust fund baby and his fund is huge. Charities are his thing. This was some 'Save the Seven Seas' do. Calypso was there, wearing the pearls. Lady admired them. I suppose that's why Rawlings stole them and tried to gift them to Lady. Or maybe he just liked the danger of trying. From what I know of him, Rawlings is easily bored and a fan of danger. Breaks up the monotony of being insufferably rich, I suppose."

I laughed under my breath without humor.

Drew seized the moment. "Your turn."

"I doubt I have much to offer. This is my first day on the job."

"Time's running out," Drew said. "Ms. Califia's hedging her bets bringing on one more. It's Hail Mary pass time."

That seemed right. Funny that she'd go through the whole interview process, complete with fake demon abductions. Though maybe Miranda was right when she said the godly get bored. As long as I got paid, I didn't much care what she did for entertainment providing it didn't inconvenience me.

"My first stop was Michael's sister," I said, "and if the family is rich, it only barely shows in her case."

Drew held up a finger to stop me. "Michael is rich. The sister hardly got anything when the last parent died."

"Why was that?"

Drew shrugged. "Daddy was a bastard. Very old school. He thought women should marry rich, not be independently wealthy themselves. He thought Miranda's job in life was specifically to marry well and produce heirs for the Rawlings empire."

"That wasn't Michael's job, too?"

"Michael's job is to sow his wild oats until he's forty, then take the reins. Heirs are a bonus, but that job was primarily handed to Miranda."

I seriously disliked Michael Rawlings's father.

"Michael's sister sent me to Kimiko," I said and had a thought. "Did you know that his sister's a witch? A rather powerful one."

He spooned up a healthy bit of soup. "I did. And it's an interesting fact about her."

"Because?"

"Because Daddy died under mysterious circumstances and I've wondered if the witch-daughter had anything to do with it."

"What sort of mysterious circumstances?"

"His racing yacht, which he was sailing solo that day, sunk for no reason that anyone can ascertain, and he drowned. He definitely wasn't suicidal."

I pondered that. Miranda had a temper and her flight or fight instinct skewed to fight. Had Daddy told her what was in his will and it'd pissed her off enough to sink his boat?

If she had or hadn't killed her father wasn't any of my concern. My concern was finding and returning Calypso's necklace. Still, it was something to keep in mind in case I came up against her again.

"Is Michael a witch?" I said.

Drew shook his head. "Not that I know of. Anything's possible though." He shot me an encouraging smile "Go on. Miranda sent you to Kimiko. What did Kimiko have to say?"

"That she'd seen the necklace and that Michael didn't like that she'd seen it. The day she peeked at what Michael had in his pocket was the last time she saw him. She tried calling him, but his number had been disconnected."

My *pho* was growing cold. I squeezed a lime over the soup and took another spoonful. I looked back up at Drew. "Are you going to give me the girlfriend list so I can visit them myself?"

"Sure. But none of them had anything useful to say. None of them have seen or heard from Michael since he took the necklace. But your information that Kimiko actually saw the pearls and Michael didn't like it is interesting. I'm not sure what it means, if anything, other than he was careless."

I stirred some noodles around with my chopsticks. "I think it means Michael was running scared. He took the pearls to Kimiko's in hope of hiding out there. He knew Calypso knew he'd stolen her necklace and she'd sent her agents after him. He knew he couldn't go home. He knew Lady was unlikely to protect him or he would have banged on the door and tried to get inside her house."

Drew regarded me thoughtfully. "All of which means what?"

"I'm not sure," I said. "It could mean he's left the area. If it was me and the goddess of the sea was on my tail, I'd get far inland. If I thought Lady Califia wasn't happy with something I'd done, I might leave the state." I paused, thinking. "He's screwed up big time and he knows it."

"He could come and beg for forgiveness," Drew said.

I nodded, but said, "I don't think so. He doesn't seem the type from what I know of him. He's probably mystified as to how he got himself into this situation. I get the feeling he's used to things working out in his favor."

"Where do you think he is?" Drew asked. "And does he still have the pearls?"

"Those are the big questions," I said. "I don't have the answers, but I will."

Drew grinned. "Not if I get them first."

I shrugged. I could see he liked competition; it spurred him on. Me? I just wanted to do the job I was hired for. And beat the others to it.

"So," he said putting down his spoon and pushing his bowl away, "do you want to go with me to visit the last girlfriend?"

8

We took Drew's car to Girlfriend Number Five's house. I wasn't a fan of not taking two cars, but it made sense to only take one. Drew pulled to the curb a few houses down from the woman's address, turned off the engine, and cursed under his breath.

"Something wrong?" I said, because sometimes you have to say obvious things to get people to share their thoughts.

"You see those guys over there?" Drew glanced toward two tall, very good-looking men talking as they crossed the street a few houses from where we parked.

"Yeah," I said.

"Remember I told you there was a partnered pair on the trail of the necklace? That's them. People call them Friday and Saturday because they're always next to each other. Do you know them?"

I watched the pair walk toward a car. One of the men had his keys out and was beeping the door open. I was memorizing both men's features.

"Heard of them, but don't know them."

Drew nodded. "I trained Finn for the job; he's Friday.

Stefan—Saturday—is psychic. A useful trick in our business."

I'd already figured out that Drew was probably gay. The wistfulness look that crossed his face made me think Friday had been more than a trainee.

He pushed his door open but looked over his shoulder at me. "You don't seem to know many people."

I pushed my door open as well since it seemed pretty obvious we were going to go talk to Friday and Saturday. "As I said, I work alone."

I wasn't opposed to temporary partnerships though. I'd teamed up with others in the past and probably would again. Permanent partners, though, weren't my thing.

Drew was out of the car and striding across the street calling in a friendly voice, "Hey. Finn. Wait up." I climbed out and followed him, catching up as he hit the sidewalk on the other side of the road.

The couple had stopped and turned at the call and waited for us.

Drew and Finn bro-hugged stiffly and briefly when we reached them. Andrew gave Saturday a tight smile and a nod of greeting. Both men had given me the once-over and evidently approved since Saturday stuck out his hand and said, "Hi. I'm Stefan and this is Finn."

"Shay Greene," I said, taking his hand and giving back the same firmness of grip he'd given me.

Drew broke into all the polite introductions. "You've been to see Tabby Fontaine," making it a statement not a question. "You mind sharing what she had to say?"

"Nothing worth the time it took," Finn said dismissively. "Tabby doesn't know anything more than anyone else seems to about where Michael Rawlings might be."

"Isn't tabby a kind of cat?" I said, to lighten the mood and get Friday and Saturday on our side a bit.

Finn chortled under his breath. "It's short for Tabitha, though her hair is yellow and brown striped. Maybe she's a cat shifter."

I laughed a little too. At least this Finn guy had a sense of humor. Drew, so far, hadn't shown he was anything but work, which was fine with me.

Drew moved his attention to Stefan, he of the psychic abilities. "Is Tabby a shifter? Or a magical of any sort?"

Stefan shook his head. "I don't think so. Other than Lady Califia, Michael Rawlings seemed to like his women completely human and vanilla-plain."

I stowed that bit of information away. Michael Rawlings saw the goddess of California as a prize worth winning but spent his time with *ordin* women—the unmagical. He likely thought highly of himself and picked *ordin* women to reinforce his self-perception. The type who set his sights high, feeling that was what he deserved, but enjoyed dabbling in 'the lower depths' with women he could feel superior to.

Not only did I not like Michael Rawlings' father, I didn't like Michael Rawlings in the least. Which would make getting the necklace back and bringing him down all the sweeter.

We all shook hands again, and the couple turned and got into a white Prius, to head off wherever they were going next.

Where was I going next? The sister had sent me to the girlfriend, which led to more girlfriends. Drew had visited all the girlfriends except Kimiko. I'd talked to her. Friday and Saturday evidently had visited all the other girlfriends as well and seemingly gotten nothing from them. Dead ends all around, though I'd come back and talk to Tabby and the others myself. My experience with men dealing with women is that they sometimes didn't know the right questions to ask.

"That's it for the day," Drew said. "I don't know about you, but I feel like I've chased all over for nothing. I've talked to more women this week than I have in a month and I'm not one step closer to knowing where Michael Rawlings or the necklace is." He sighed heavily. "Come on. I'll take you back to your car."

Drew waited in the parking lot until I'd climbed into my car and started the engine. He gave me a cheerful good-bye wave and pulled out toward the street. I sat in my car a moment, watching him leave and thinking about what I'd learned today, which wasn't much. I'd have no good news to deliver to Lady once I got back to the house on the hill. I did want to ask about the bonus though. I'd insist it be added to my agreement.

I put the car into gear and headed toward the street. I made it almost halfway across the lot when the engine sputtered and died. My first thought was I'd messed up somehow when I'd filled the tank but a glance at the gauge told me the gas tank was full. I scowled, pulled on the emergency brake, and got out to take a look under the hood. Maybe a wire or hose had come loose. Not that I know much about cars but looking at the engine seemed like the thing to do. If that failed, I had a card for roadside assistance in my wallet and I wasn't afraid to use it.

I'd pulled up the hood and secured it in the up position with the pole that lay inside the engine compartment when a blast of wind hit me, shoving me forward. My belly hit the bottom of the engine compartment opening. It hurt.

I rubbed my belly and turned to look around. There were trees along one edge of the parking lot. Trees whose leaves and limbs weren't in motion from the strong gust that had blown by only moments ago. I felt magic in the air. Someone was making the wind happen.

Another gust hit me, pushing my back against the car this time. I summoned up air for myself, swirling a cocoon around me to stave off anything coming my way.

"I know you're there," I said, my voice no louder than if I spoke to someone standing next to me. "Step up and show yourself."

A swirl of leaves raced across the parking lot toward me. An older couple came out of the *pho* place. The swirl of leaves in the air angled around them as nimbly as a dancer. The couple gave the leaves a glance but didn't seem to find the sudden swirl out of the ordinary. They continued past me and got into an old white minivan.

The wind died the moment the older couple was tucked into their car. The twirling leaves fell to the ground. A stocky man in his forties, a few inches taller than me, and wearing loose black trousers and a black button-up shirt stood in front of me. His dark hair was cut military short. His black eyes gleamed with what I took as malice.

"I am Saylor," the man said in a voice that could easily have been announcing an upcoming action-adventure movie. "God of the sea and sky." He put his hands on his hips and glared at me. "You will stop looking for the Mermaid's Lament stolen from Calypso."

I'd been flabbergasted by Lady's announcement that she was a goddess. This man's pronouncement made me want to laugh. Instead I said, "Mermaid's Lament?"

He sniffed. "The string of aubergine pearls stolen by Michael Rawlings."

Kimiko had said pearls were sometimes called 'mermaid's tears.' Evidently Calypso's necklace had so many tears it was a full-on lament. The necklace having its own name probably meant the pearls had special properties to warrant that title.

I shook my head slightly. "Give me a good reason why I shouldn't try to recover the sea goddess's necklace and I'll consider it."

The self-proclaimed god looked thrown for a moment. I guessed he hadn't expected that kind of response.

"Because I command it," he said. "And if you don't, I'll make sure you're very sorry you made that decision."

A great blast of wind buffeted me, overcoming the cocoon I'd built but had let whither since the god had appeared. I was knocked back a couple of steps but caught myself. This 'god' making his point.

I summoned up air and sent an even stronger blast back at him. He stumbled but didn't fall. When he'd steadied himself, he grinned.

"Like to fight, do you?" he said, and sent a long wave of wind toward me.

"Not all that much," I muttered, but I wouldn't back down.

My protective cocoon was back up at full strength. His blast hit my air and parted, swirling to either side. I felt it battering the sides of my cocoon, but it couldn't penetrate through to me. I summoned up fire, rolled it into a ball, and flung the flaming mass toward him.

He ducked. The fireball sailed over his head and landed on a patch of asphalt where, fortunately, no car was parked. The asphalt hissed and liquefied. The arid small of it burning filled the air.

He pulled up straight and sent an even larger ball of fire at me. I whirled away to the side, throwing another fireball as I turned. His fireball flew past me and hit a concrete streetlamp. Mine hit a small pile of trash some idiot had left lying on the ground. The trash burst into flames. I quickly summoned rain to put out the fire.

We couldn't go on like this. There were people in the pho place who could come out at any moment, and any second a new car could drive into the lot. Some innocent bystander could get hurt.

I held up my hands. "No more. You win."

His disbelief was clear on his face. "Just like that?" He narrowed his eyes. "I don't believe you."

"This is a public place. We keep fighting here and someone besides you could be hurt. So, again—tell me one good reason why I shouldn't try to recover the necklace and I'll drive straight up to my boss and quit this job."

He blinked. I could practically see the slow turn of the gears in his brain as he adjusted to this new reality.

"Because I tell you to," he said.

I chortled. "Not even close to good."

He drew in a deep breath and let it out. "Because Lady Califia is lying to you. She has no intention of returning the necklace. The pearls have magical powers. No matter who possesses them, if they put the necklace around someone's throat and pronounce a few innocent sounding words, that person will be forever enslaved. She can't be allowed that sort of power. She'll only abuse it. Starting, probably, with you."

I watched his face, trying to judge how much of what he said was true and how much was utter bullshit. If only I were psychic like my new acquaintance, Saturday. How much easier things must be when you can delve into your opponent's mind. I had to go on my gut and what I sensed. My sense said there was more going on here than I'd been led to believe. My gut said there was a smidge of truth in his claim, but not much more than a smidge.

"That's a damn good reason," I said, mollifying him. And then I lied. "I'll drop my search."

He nodded. "Excellent. Good doing business with you."

The leaves that had lain quiet on the ground whirled up again into a small tornado and zipped away, carrying the man with them.

I stood a moment longer considering what he'd said. Were the pearls magic in the way he claimed? Would Lady abuse that power? Miranda seemed to think Lady wasn't to be trusted. Was Miranda giving me fair warning or just throwing out words to make me distrust my boss? I had nothing but gut sense and feelings to go on to any of those questions. And right now, my gut was as confused and unsure as my brain was.

I got in my car and turned the key. It started right up.

9

*L*ady's face clouded as she listened to my story of being confronted by the god of the sea and sky. She huffed an annoyed breath when I finished.

We sat on her veranda. To the west, the sky was a brilliant pineapple-yellow and glowing carnelian show of sundown. It would be dark soon. When I woke in the morning, there would be only three days left before Calypso would send ocean water flooding over the land.

"She sent Saylor after you, did she?" Lady said. "Calypso thinks she's so cleaver with names. Saylor's father was a Navy sailor, so Saylor with a y instead of an i." Lady stood and paced across the veranda and back. "But why? What does Calypso gain if Saylor injures you?" She stopped and faced me. "Was he trying to injure you or merely frighten you?"

"Both, I'd say."

Lady's lips pressed together. "Humph. Why would Calypso want you injured? Saylor would never think on his own to attack you. He would have come only by her orders, unless he's gone rogue."

Her voice dropped low, as if her next remarks were meant

only for herself. "The god of sea and sky, my ass. He's a demigod at best. I wonder if his mother knows he's running around presenting himself as a god. Calypso would not be pleased by that, not one bit."

She refocused on me. "Do you know the sea goddess? Have you crossed her somehow?"

I shook my head.

"Well," Lady said, "there's certainly a reason behind it all. It's late. Perhaps we should sleep on it and revisit the question in the morning. I'll call the other hunters and ask if any of them were confronted. If yes, then we know something we didn't know before. If not, then we know something different that was unknown until now, and I will be able to warn the others to be on their guards."

I took the moment to ask some of the questions I wanted answers to.

"How many hunters are searching for the necklace? Besides me."

Lady had turned away and was reaching for her phone. She turned back. Her eyes narrowed as she appraised me.

"How do you know there are other hunters, besides my having mentioned it?"

"Drew Miller told me. Plus, I ran into Friday and Saturday at one of the places I'd gone to ask questions."

Lady made a scoffing sound. "Drew can never keep his mouth shut. I don't know why I continue to employ him."

"So how many? How much competition do I have?"

"There are five, four if you consider Finn and Stefan as one, since they're a pair."

That matched what Drew had said.

"Drew told me something else. He said he'd been promised a bonus if he brought in the necklace."

"And you want to know why no bonus was offered to

you. Because you are new. I only offer a bonus to hunters who have proven their worth in the past."

"That's a bit unfair," I said. "If I bring in the prize, I should get the full reward. Your other searchers have been at it longer and found nothing concrete. It makes sense for you to incentivize me to the same extent as the others. It doesn't make sense, now that I know about the bonus, for you to refuse it and yet expect me to work at the top of my game."

Lady studied me before she spoke. "Consider this an internship. Do well and more jobs, and perhaps bonuses, will come your way."

I shook my head. "I don't work that way."

Lady pressed her lips together, thinking, I assumed, before she answered. "Perhaps you have a point. Go to bed now. I'll think it over and give you my decision in the morning."

She rang a bell that sat on the little outdoor table. Mr. Beefy, the butler or whatever he was, appeared. Drew had told me his name, but it was gone from my memory.

"Show Shayna to her room, please."

I remained sitting. "Another question. Is what Saylor claimed true?"

Lady scoffed. "Which part? That the pearls can be used to enslave anyone who wears them or that I plan to use them that way?"

"Either," I said. "Both."

She laughed quietly under her breath. "You give it some thought and then trust your instincts. I'm sure you'll come to the right conclusion."

She turned away from me and stared at where the sky was turning dark blue and gray, and the first stars were beginning to glimmer.

I picked up the J.C. Penny and CVS shopping bags that

contained what were currently all my worldly goods and followed Mr. Beefy into the house.

The room Lady had given me was huge with a spectacular view of the ocean over the hilltops. Again, I wouldn't see the surf crashing on the shore or hear it from this distance, but now, at night with the curtains open, I marveled at the lights embracing the curve of Santa Monica Bay, what the real estate people called The Queen's Necklace. The way the room and windows faced, I'd be able to see a sliver of the lights even from the bed. I cracked the windows open and heard crickets slowly chirping in the spring night. The scent of something floral, sweet, and night blooming trickled in on the slight breeze. I could get used to this. Providing that Lady didn't out to be some madwoman with dreams of controlling people—me—with the Mermaid's Lament.

The bed was king-sized, with a fluffy blue comforter, and ensconced in a four-poster frame. The wood was something dark, dense, and tightly grained. Beyond that, I wasn't a big expert on wood types even though wood was friendly to me. There was a dresser in the same wood, a small writing desk with a comfortable chair upholstered in black leather, and a huge walk-in closet. I looked at the two shopping bags that held my belongings and laughed. Even if I had every piece of clothing and all the shoes and purses I owned here with me, they wouldn't begin to fill a quarter of that closet.

The ensuite bathroom was bigger than my bedroom at home, with a glassed-in shower with a view out to the bay. There weren't any houses nearby and since Lady's house was on the hilltop, no one could look down into the shower, but I still didn't think I'd be comfortable using it. I'd have to eventually. Couldn't go about my business stinky. Morning would be soon enough to try it out.

Staring out a window at the Queen's Necklace, I wondered why Saylor had tried to frighten me off today, if that's what the attempt was. Calypso had demanded her necklace be returned. It didn't make sense for her son to try to stop that from happening, unless Saylor wanted to see California flooded all the way to the San Andreas Fault. But why would he want that? Some grudge he had against Lady?

Was Saylor telling the truth: the pearls were magical, and Lady wanted them for their power to enslave whomever she chose? I'd think that if Lady were that sort of person, some rumor of it would have surfaced by now. Her life was scrutinized down to what color her toenails were painted when she attended an opening.

Except no rumor of her magic or, for pity's sake, her *goddessness*, had surfaced that I was aware of and I'd researched her pretty thoroughly before coming to the interview, because I like to be prepared.

There might be magic in the necklace, but I didn't think it was what Saylor claimed, or that Lady was who Saylor accused her of being. Why? Purely instinct. I'd keep a sharp eye out though, just in case.

I yanked the tags off the new pajamas I'd bought, put them on and crawled into bed. The sheets were as soft as kitten fur. I couldn't even guess at how high the thread count was. The pillows were just the right amount of hardness. I pulled the down comforter up under my chin but couldn't quite relax

I sat up, fished around for my phone, and dialed Darci's cell phone number.

"It's me," I said when she answered. "How's the drying out of my house coming along?"

"Oh," Darci said and sighed. "It's coming but it's slow. Where are staying? The hotel where your friend works?"

"No," I said, fatigue settling over me. "I'm staying with at my new employer's house. She has an extra room."

"Is that a good idea, Shay?" Worry was clear in her voice. "How well do you know this person?"

I smiled to myself. Darci and Bella had a tendency to be overprotective of me. "Well enough to know she probably isn't a crazed murderer who will knife me in the night."

Darci huffed a breath. "All right, Shay. I know you think Bella and I worry too much about you, but the truth is we worry the exact right amount. You take care of yourself."

"I will," I said. "Kiss Bella for me and you both sleep tight. I'll talk to you tomorrow."

We hung up. I snuggled down under the comforter and closed my eyes.

I shivered as I stepped from the sunshine into the shadows the trees cast, but not from the sudden chill. I shivered because woods scared me. Nothing good ever happened in the woods. Mean witches who ate children lived there. I knew because Mommy read me the story. Hansel and Gretel escaped, but what about all the children before them? Maybe there were other witches there. Ones that hadn't wound up in their own stewpot.

But the singing drew me on, deeper and deeper into the trees.

I burst suddenly into a clearing. A woman with skin the color of red grapes and wearing a silver headband walked up to me and reached out her hand. I was scared, but I took it. Her skin was sun warmed and soft. She pulled me close and bent down to whisper in my ear.

"Never forget," she said in a voice as deep and strong as a church bell, "When we ask, you will say, Yes."

I awoke shaking. Say yes to what?

10

Mr. Beefy rapped politely on my door and called, "Are you awake?"

The morning sun streamed through the big picture window with the spectacular view of Santa Monica Bay.

I hauled myself out of the very comfortable bed and opened the door enough to peek out.

"Lady would like you to join her for breakfast in thirty minutes," he said, then turned and sauntered off.

Time to try that open-to-the-world shower, I guessed.

Clean and clothed in a new t-shirt, my old jeans, new socks, and my old shoes, I made my way down the long hall toward the front of the house. As I passed an open door, I glanced in and saw Lady seated at a small, square dining table.

The 'breakfast room,' as I thought of it, was large and airy with walls the color of morning sunshine in August. This room faced easterly, so no ocean view. Instead, large windows framed a garden beyond filled with flowers and herbs. This was a different garden than the one visible from the veranda. I recognized yarrow, catmint, lavender, and rose-mary. There were more plants that I couldn't name. I'd never been much of a flower person, and the only ones I saw that I recognized were roses in various hues.

Lady sat at a table built from a light-colored wood. (I could see the legs beneath the tablecloth that covered the top.) There were only two chairs. Was Mr. Beefy her usual breakfast companion? The table was more than large enough for three chairs. Lady had excluded him this morning on purpose, I thought. Or maybe he always ate alone in the kitchen while Lady ate alone in the breakfast room, and an extra chair had been brought in for my benefit. Curiosity made me wonder about their relationship. Courtesy kept me from speculating overmuch. Whatever the relationship was, it was their business and so long as it didn't interfere with me doing my job, I didn't care.

Lady spotted me at the doorway and motioned for me to join her.

"You slept well?" she said when I'd taken the chair opposite her.

"Very," I said.

She poured tea into a delicate white cup trimmed with gold without asking if I wanted any. "Good."

I sipped the tea. Light yellow this morning, unlike the green tea yesterday, with a strong scent of lemon and ginger.

Mr. Beefy came in carrying a silver tea tray with two plates filled with scrambled eggs and bacon. He set one plate in front of Lady and one in front of me.

"Thank you, Edwin," she said, dismissing him.

Right. Mr. Beefy's first name was Edwin. Drew had told me that. The name didn't suit him though. He should have been named Tristan or Alejandro, something faintly foreign and exotic to go along with his spectacular looks.

Lady took a forkful of scrambled eggs, chewed and swallowed them. I ate a forkful of my own. The eggs were scrumptious. I detected cream cheese along with butter, salt, and pepper. I took another bite and wondered if Edwin was cook as well as butler and general factotum.

When she'd finished a few bites from her plate, Lady daintily patted her lips with a cream-colored linen napkin and set the napkin back on her lap.

"I've been pondering the mystery of why Saylor attacked you yesterday," she said.

I paused the forkful of eggs that was on its way to my mouth. "Did you reach a conclusion?"

"No," Lady said.

Well that was disappointing.

"So," Lady said, "it seems the only thing to do is for us to go ask Calypso why she sent him."

"Us?" I said. "I'd planned to interview the rest of Michael's girlfriends today."

Lady waved off that idea with a flick of her hand. "The other hunters have spoken with the girlfriends. There's little if anything to be gained there for you. I want you to accompany me to speak with Calypso."

She might be right, but all the other hunters were men. I could talk to the girlfriends woman to woman, and that often made a difference. But Lady was the boss. If she wanted me to go with her to meet Calypso, so be it.

In the past couple of days, I'd met a goddess and a demigod. Today looked like *meet goddess number two* day. A goddess who wasn't all that chummy with my boss and who probably had sent her son to try to scare me. Oh joy.

"She's the goddess of the sea," I said. "Do we take a boat?"

Lady nibbled on a piece of bacon before she answered.

"Yes, as a matter of fact. I've arranged to meet her on Catalina Island. She likes a neutral ground, as do I."

As it happens, I like boats and being on the water. It looked like a lovely day to be at sea. At least part of today's work might be pleasant.

I returned to eating the really delicious scrambled eggs. Edwin, if it was Edwin who'd made these, could cook, that was plain.

"No bacon?" Lady said. "It's quite good. The hogs are fed a diet of acorns, hickory nuts, and organic fruits and vegetables on my ranch in Sonoma County."

I smiled thinly and shrugged slightly. "Vegetarian. I eat eggs and butter, but not meat."

"Oh," Lady said, clearly surprised. "I'll let Edwin know."

"Thank you," I said.

Lady looked at me over the slice of bacon she still held. "Did you decide if Saylor was telling the truth or a lie about the pearls and about me?"

"I did," I said.

"And?"

"And I'm here, eating breakfast with you."

"Good," Lady said, and sunk her teeth into the bacon slice.

After breakfast Mr. Beefy—Edwin—drove Lady and me to the pier in San Pedro in Lady's bright red Tesla. I was happy to see she was green in her car choice. I wasn't fanatical about being good to the planet, but I tried to do my bit here and there. I was vegetarian not so much because I was opposed to eating animals, I wasn't, but I did think the way we ranched was often cruel and almost always wasteful.

I choose not to contribute. I ate organic as much as possible for the same 'be nice to the planet' reason. What others did was their business.

I thought we'd take the Catalina Express ship that could get you from San Pedro to Avalon on Catalina Island in an hour. Or maybe, since money wasn't an issue with Lady, we'd take the helicopter over.

Instead, Lady led us to where the private boats were moored. She stepped into a long, sleek, blue hulled speed boat that would have felt right at home in the old Miami Vice television show. I had no idea what kind it was, but it looked like it was going a hundred miles an hour while sitting quietly in its slip.

Edwin followed Lady onto the boat, then turned and offered his hand to help me aboard. I took it, stepped into the fiberglass and chrome showcase, and settled into one of the contoured seats that looked like they could have been on the deck of a star cruiser. Lady took the seat behind the wheel. Edwin sat beside her. I was perfectly content to be in the second row, since I was pretty sure a lot of spray would be coming up over the bow once we got going. I'm a tad embarrassed to admit I looked for a seatbelt. Of course there wasn't one, nor did Lady or Edwin put on or offer me a life vest. Maybe Lady, being a goddess, and Edwin, being under her protection, didn't have to worry about drowning. I was a good swimmer, but not strong enough to swim to shore if we capsized ten miles out.

We putt-putted our way out of the channel and into open water. Lady turned and looked at me over her shoulder.

"Do you like speed boats?" she asked.

"I prefer sailboats," I said, being honest. "They're quiet and don't pollute the sea as much."

Lady looked slightly amused at my not-so-subtle dig. "I

have one of those, too. I'll take you sailing some time." A slight crease formed in her forehead. "Are you useful on a sailboat, or just a ride-along?"

"Useful," I said.

Lady nodded and turned back around. Seconds later we were tearing across the water toward Catalina Island, the bow rising out of the water like a rearing horse.

About ten minutes out and almost half-way to Catalina I was wet enough from spray shooting over the bow and leaping up from the boat's sides to start wishing I had something to dry off with. As if he'd read my mind, Mr. Bee—Edwin—reached below his chair and sat back up holding a fluffy, blue hand-towel that he handed to me.

The towel had an anchor and the words *Lady Califia* embroidered with gold thread on it. I laughed under my breath. No one ever said Lady was shy and humble. I dabbed at my face, but no sooner got one part dry than it was wet again. Still, it was nice to have something to try to dry off with.

I stopped in mid-dry-off and crumpled the towel in my hand. A frisson of nerves shot up my breastbone. Something wasn't right here.

I thought Edwin felt it, too. He grabbed Lady's arm, leaned over and said something that looked pretty urgent from the angle of his body and the look on what I could see of his face. I raised myself in my chair and scanned the ocean as best I could.

My heart froze, then pumped like crazy. A large whirlpool, not something the Pacific Ocean around here was known for, spun wildly directly in front of us, sucking water down deep into its vortex. I didn't think it had been there moments earlier.

Lady shoved the boat into reverse, but the bow was

already caught in the edge of the spinning ocean. Her hands squeezed tight around the wheel. I couldn't see her face, but my guess was her eyes were wide and her teeth clamped together in concentration. Adrenaline had to be pumping through her as surely and as strongly as it pumped through me. I grabbed the edges of my chair.

The bow careened to the left. The boat's stern over swung, sending us spinning in a full circle. Water gushed up from all directions, drenching the three of us. I clung to the edge of the seat for all I was worth. Getting thrown out of the boat into that maelstrom wasn't an experience I wanted. I needed to calm these mad waters before any or all of us were thrown out of the boat. I was used to controlling the elements on land—not at sea, not in the midst of being spun around like we were on a wild carnival ride.

Calm focus. Still the waters.

Yeah, right.

The eddy grabbed the bow again and we started a second spin. I clutched the seat edges as the force of the turn threw me to the side. I put one hand on the slick, wet gunwale and pushed myself back into sitting upright. In front of me, Edwin had been flung sideways as well and had levered himself back up the same way I had. He didn't look scared, only frustrated—as though he desperately wanted to do something but didn't know how.

We'd spun halfway around with the bow facing away from the whirlpool when I centered myself enough to use my control of water to slow the whirlpool's spin.

As the water directly behind us began to calm, the water in front of us roiled and began to foam. I switched my attention and calmed those waters. The ocean on either side pushed us first one-way and then another.

Every time I calmed a bit of ocean, another burst into

turbulent life. I'd never run into anything like this. I could make water do my bidding. I closed my eyes and concentrated hard. The mad spinning and jostling lessened. Some force fought my magic, trying to stir the waters again. I gripped my hands into fists and threw my magic into the sea with all my might.

The boat was suddenly as still as if it were becalmed; the only motion a slight bobbing on the current.

Lady gunned the engines. My eyes flew open. The bow rose until the boat was approaching perpendicular and I was sure we were going to tip all the way over. Somehow Lady made the boat pivot and we raced away from the reforming vortex.

We kept going, heading away from the spinning water, and back toward the California shore until Lady turned the boat in a wide arc that swung around the whirlpool and headed us once again toward Catalina Island.

My heart beat fast against my ribs. My feet were in several inches of water we'd taken on while fighting the maelstrom. We were out of danger, but adrenaline still raced through my blood.

Lady's shout was so loud I heard it over the engines. "That fucking, lying bitch!"

Edwin turned and looked over his shoulder at me. I gave him the best *I'm okay* smile I could manage.

My smile vanished. *Something* was rising from the water directly in front of us.

11

I blinked to clear my brain and looked again. It was still there—a smooth, gray island rising from the ocean. As it rose, eyes as black as oil and as large as Volkswagens appeared—eyes that were laser-focused on us little humans in our puny boat. I glanced around in a panic. There were no other boats in sight. We were on our own.

Edwin leapt from his chair and over the windscreen to the bow. He looked tiny compared to the creature watching us with cold, unblinking eyes. A long, thick harpoon with evil-looking barbs on the end appeared in his hand. I had no idea how he'd done that. He cocked his arm, readying for a throw.

Lady had throttled down the engine, the sound quieting to a leopard roar. The boat bucked and wobbled, the ocean stirred up by the beast's rise. Edwin had his legs bent at the knees and his feet spread wide apart to give him some stability. He'd shucked off his shoes in some moment I hadn't noticed. One bare foot was planted on each of the two grip strips that ran the length of the bow. Even with the grip strips, it'd take amazing balance for him not to be thrown off. If he was wishing for a life vest, it didn't show in the confident way he stood.

His confidence helped quell my panicking heart. I stood, keeping one hand on the chair for balance, and summoned my power over water to quiet the ocean as much as possible.

It's not easy for me to manage two elements at once, but I did my best to split my concentration, restraining the ocean with half my mind while calling up fire with the other half. Fire for the beast.

The beast kept rising, the tops of long, massive arms beginning to show. The tip of one octopus-like arm with suckers as wide as dinner plates snaked from the water into the air. The boat rocked from side to side in the wake stirred up by the creature. I readied fire while keeping my gaze locked on Edwin. When he threw the harpoon, aiming for the creature's left eye, I flung fire at its right eye.

Edwin's throw missed its target. The harpoon hung like a wooden tear from the beast's cheek. My fire had found its mark. The creature roared and thrashed. The water around us churned. The boat tipped, dropping the left-side gunwales into the water. Edwin lost his balance and tipped toward falling. I sent a blast of air to keep him upright on the bow. He spared a nanosecond to glance at me over his shoulder then turned back to face the beast, a second harpoon now in his hand. I stopped thinking about fire and put all my focus into keeping the ocean as still as possible around the boat. The last thing we needed was Edwin falling in the water. Or the boat capsizing.

The beast raised an arm toward the sky and brought it down with a mighty slap. Seawater splashed high into the air. The boat rocked like a tipsy college student coming home from his first frat party.

Edwin windmilled his arms as his balance failed. I sent air to push him back to center. He didn't bother to glance at me this time. He cocked his arm back to throw another harpoon that had again magically appeared in his hand.

The beast's sucker-covered arm rose again, joined by a second arm on the other side of the creature's body. Edwin yelled as he heaved the harpoon toward the beast's large, black eye. I couldn't control metal and wood like I could the elements, but they were friendly to me. I sent fire to heat the harpoon's barbed tip and air to push it even faster and accurately to its target.

The harpoon struck dead center of the creature's left eye. The kraken screamed and threw its head forward into the water. The boat rocked side-to-side, the left gunwale dipping into the water, and then the right. I gripped the back of the chair as if it were the only thing between me and the deep blue sea—which it pretty much was. Lady had a firm grip on the steering wheel and was throttling the engine up and down, making small reverse and forward adjustments.

Why not just reverse hard? Get us the hell away from the kraken.

Unless the boat couldn't outrun it. Unless trying to escape would leave us more open to attack. The beast's arms were long. And I had no idea if it was fast moving through the water or what.

Our best hope was to kill it.

And maybe Lady didn't have the power to do that herself. She'd said she was a land goddess, and we were at sea. And while she could use her voice for persuasion, I'd not seen her as a fighter.

The beast raised its head from the water. Blood so dark red it was almost black streamed from the damaged eye. The eye I'd burned had turned ashy gray. The beast shook its head violently from side to side, trying to fling away the harpoon. Edwin readied another. Where were his weapons coming from? That was a question for later. I shifted my focus from calming the waters to sending air to keep Edwin from falling over or sliding off the bow, and then again to the water. Shifting my attention back and forth wasn't letting me do either as well as I'd have liked, but the boat rocked less as the water calmed, and Edwin kept his footing.

Maybe he figured out I'd helped a bit with that last harpoon thrust because he glanced over his shoulder at me and nodded slightly before straightening and throwing the weapon toward the beast's already-burned eye. I again sent fire to the barbed tip and wind behind the shaft to shove it forward.

The beast screamed as the metal and wood drove into its eye. I wanted the spear to pierce its brain. I wanted the creature dead. I pushed the harpoon with wind until it disappeared, buried deep in the kraken's head.

The beast thrashed. The waters churned like they were being stirred by a giant eggbeater. I'd forgotten about Edwin in the few seconds it took to push the spear further into the beast. His yell brought my attention back to him, but I couldn't ready wind fast enough to catch him as he flailed in the air. His fall into the water didn't raise enough splash to be noticed in the mad roiling sea.

Lady jumped up, ran to the back of the boat and grabbed a long grappling pole. She leaned out over the side of the boat, extending the pole out as far as she could toward him. The boat began to turn on its own, the crazy current pushing it stern first toward the beast.

"Grab the wheel," Lady yelled. "Straighten us out and then make little adjustments to keep us steady."

I crawled between the seats and took the chair Lady had vacated. I didn't know shit about how to steer a powerboat but thought it couldn't be all that different from sail. I took the wheel and with the engine only slightly more than idling, managed to bring her around so the side faced where Edwin was trying his best to swim to the boat. I made tiny adjustments as Lady had said and set my focus to settling the waters at least long enough to get Edwin back on board.

The beast was slapping all eight of its arms on the water. Waves rose and fell. Spray slapped me in the face. I wiped it away from my eyes with the back of my hand. If I weren't also calming the waters as best I could, all three of us would be in the ocean by now and probably drowned.

Edwin had gotten hold of the grappling pole and was pulling himself hand-over-hand to the side of the boat. Lady was straining to hold the pole with one hand and pull him up side of the boat with the other. I gritted my teeth and focused on the water around Edwin, making a waterspout. I gave it all I had. The waterspout propelled him into the air. Lady caught him in midair and yanked him onto the boat. He landed with a hard thud.

The beast was losing steam, flailing less, and slowly sinking from view.

"That thing will pull us down with it if it can," Lady said as she pushed me out of the captain's chair.

I'd already figured that out and was again working my magic on the water.

She took the seat and revved the engine. In a move I would have called impossible if I hadn't seen it myself, the boat stood on its stern, bow in the air, and spun like a ballerina. The bow slammed back down on the water, rattling my teeth. Lady gunned the engine. The boat sped away from the last gasps of the dying creature.

I could see Lady cursing under her breath. I was in the chair next to her now, while Edwin had taken the seat I'd occupied before. I leaned close, to listen to what she was muttering.

"You cheating, two-faced bitch, Calypso, hear me good. You will pay for this betrayal, and you will pay dearly."

12

I mentally held my breath the rest of the way to Catalina Island, but no further uproars disturbed the trip. I thought we might moor in Avalon Bay, where the tourist ships came in and most people who came in their own boats stayed. It was on the side of the island closest to the California shore and had plenty of mooring spots. Instead Lady pointed the boat to run up the island's rugged coastline.

Edwin was back in the seat next to Lady and I'd returned to the seat behind him. He turned to face me. "We'll meet Calypso at Rippers Cove. Do you know it?"

I shook my head.

"It's isolated. Accessible only by boat," he said. "Given what happened on the way here, be on your guard."

I rubbed my hands against my thighs, as if that could calm the nerves tingling in me. Yesterday Saylor had tried to hurt me. Today a presumably sent-by-Calypso whirlpool and then a sea monster had tried to kill all three of us. For the pearls, presumably. If the Mermaid's Lament wasn't magic, what was so special about the necklace that someone would be willing to kill to keep us from finding it?

Rippers Cove, it turned out, was a narrow crescent of sandy beach that quickly became craggy hillside at the sides and back. There were no mooring buoys. I wondered if Lady planned to anchor and we'd swim to the shore, or if she meant to run her very expensive, fiberglass hulled speedboat up onto the beach.

The latter, it seemed.

She pointed the boat directly at the midpoint of the narrow beach and gunned the engines. I hunched my shoulders in surprise as cold seawater hit me from behind. I turned and saw that the huge twine engines had lifted out of the water and now stuck out from the back of the boat above the waterline. Water flying off the propellers as the engines came out of the water had soaked my upper back, neck, and the back of my head. The engines were still working, now using some kind of propulsion to thrust the boat toward the shore. If Batman or James Bond had a speedboat, I imagined it would be something like Lady's, but probably not as nice.

We hit the shore with a sudden shudder and bounced the rest of the way until almost the entire fifty feet of boat lay on the beach. Lady and Edwin calmly climbed out onto the sand while I was still sitting a little goggle-eyed from the 'landing' experience. Edwin took a few steps back, turned to me and held out his hand. I took it gratefully and let him help me to the sand.

Lady stood with one hand on her hip, the other hand pushing through her dark hair that somehow still looked perfect even after all we'd been through while she surveyed the beach and the surrounding hills.

I took a look around as well. The cove wasn't large, the beach not terribly long and strewn with large rocks and boulders to the back and sides of where we stood. The hill behind the beach sloped up quickly but looked climbable for maybe twenty feet. Then a climber would hit a sheer cliff face maybe another twenty-five to thirty feet high. Getting over that in a hurry would be a problem.

I kept looking, surveying where we were, checking possible escape routes, possible routes for danger. There was a spot where cliff and hillside met the sand. Anyone coming from above would have to be part mountain goat to reach the beach without being heard or sending small landslides down the hill. Anyone trying to escape the beach by land would have to go up the hill the same way. A wind at your back could help with speed. And if you had control over earth, you might be able to create an easy, foot-sure path for escape or a slippery, rocky, crumbling path for anyone attacking.

I wondered how long it would take one, two, or all three of us to push Lady's boat back into the water, get on board, get the engines down and running, turn the boat around and race away from Rippers Cove if that became necessary. I thought we could do it quickly enough to escape any danger from above unless they were armed. Those firing from above always had the advantage. I didn't see any way to defend us from an attack from the water except by magic.

I turned and swung my head to observe as much of the open ocean around us as I could. There were no other boats or crafts headed this way. So how was Calypso going to get here?

I laughed at myself under my breath. Calypso was the goddess of the sea. She wouldn't arrive in an ordinary boat. She'd swim up. Or be carried to shore by dolphins. Or maybe another of her sea monsters would cradle her gently in its impossibly long arms and deposit her on the shore. Anything seemed possible.

Lady stepped up beside me and together we stared at the ocean.

"She won't be coming in a boat, if that's what you're looking for," Lady said.

I nodded. "I'd figured that out. I was musing on how she might arrive. On a dolphin's back? Riding in a net pulled by whales?"

Lady raised her eyebrows. "You do have quite an imagination."

I shrugged. "I find it a benefit in my line of work. The more scenarios you can imagine, the better prepared you can be."

Lady's mouth bent in a humorless smile. "You may not be too far off. Calypso does like to make a dramatic entrance."

A school of flying fish leapt suddenly from the water about twenty feet in front of us. The leaping fish batted their fins like tiny little wings as they soared over the water, and then dove back into the sea. Wave after wave of them flew parallel to the shore.

"Is this the announcement she's coming?" I said.

Lady nodded, her tension visible in the loose fists her hands made. "I'd say so."

The flying fish were followed by leaping pods of white-sided dolphins.

Next came the sea goddess herself striding straight toward where we stood, rising slowly from the water, emerging a little more with each step—the crown of her head, her head and neck, her shoulders and bare breasts, her waist and bare hips, her legs down to her ankles.

I didn't think the water was that shallow, even this close to shore. She had to be standing on mantis rays or levitating herself…or something.

Calypso was fair skinned with long, wet, red hair that cascaded over her shoulders and down her back. Water dripped from her body, but dried as she walked toward us.

Lady had crossed her arms loosely over her chest, the way one might do while waiting for an exasperating child to be done with their foolishness.

The sea goddess smiled as she glided—not stepped—from the water and onto the land. Lady and I stood close to the waterline. Calypso stopped as soon as her feet hit dry sand.

"Welcome, Lady!" she said and spread her arms wide.

"Are you surprised we made it here?" Lady said coolly.

Calypso blinked but never lost her composure. "Why would I be surprised? This is the agreed upon place at the agreed upon time."

Lady tightened her arms over her chest ever so slightly. "A grand entrance and a fake friendly greeting won't wash away your actions, Calypso."

The sea goddess held out a hand to Lady. "I can see you're angry, but I honestly don't know about what."

Lady appraised her a long moment. "Let me begin with your son."

13

*L*ady related the story I'd told her of Saylor attacking me in the parking lot. I could hear her anger rising as she spoke and see it in the way she leaned aggressively toward the sea goddess.

"Why," Lady demanded, "did you order your son to attack my employee? And why, after I agreed in good faith to come here to meet with you, did you try twice to kill us on the way over? Answer me now."

Calypso shook her head slightly. I couldn't tell whether it was to indicate she'd not done it or that she thought either Lady or Saylor were fools.

"I have no idea what you're talking about," the sea goddess said.

I couldn't get a sense of the sea goddess. She sounded truly perplexed, but she could be a practiced liar. Lady certainly didn't seem to believe her innocent act.

Lady sneered. "The whirlpool that tried to suck us down? The Kraken that failed to drown us?"

Calypso looked honestly perplexed. Lady looked seriously pissed. This was getting us nowhere.

I took a step toward the sea goddess. "Is Saylor likely to attack me or attack our boat on his own?"

Lady's eyes flashed with momentary anger. I didn't know why.

Calypso regarded me with what I took to be a measure of disdain. "Never." She considered a moment. "Except he's been agitated and acting strangely since the Mermaid's Lament was stolen. It's as if the theft insulted him personally. It might have driven him to do something foolish."

Something foolish wasn't how I'd define the attacks.

"Was he in charge of the necklace's safety?" I asked, trying the one reason I could think of for Saylor to take it personally.

"No," Calypso said after a long beat. "The pearls were stolen because I filled my eyes with a man who'd filled his eyes with another."

Calypso's jaw tightened as she slanted a glance at Lady.

"You were stupid to be smitten with someone as mortal and foolish as Michael Rawlings," Lady said flatly. "Blaming me for your infatuation is just as stupid."

She turned to me. "Calypso and I met Michael at a charity event. He flattered us both and paid us a great deal of attention. He's a handsome man and I assumed Calypso was enjoying his attentions in much the same way I was, as an amusement for the moment."

I winced at the term "amusement" but from what I'd seen, the gods and goddesses regarded their relationships in a more casual light than I did.

I glanced at Calypso. Clearly, she knew where Lady's story was headed and wasn't happy about having it told. Lady, though, seemed to be enjoying herself. Whatever had angered her seemed to have passed.

"A few weeks later," Lady said, "I hosted an event at the

house. Calypso was there, and so was Michael. This time he all but ignored me and gave all of his attention to the sea goddess. At some point the two of them disappeared. I assumed Calypso had gotten lucky. We both enjoy a bit of 'mundane' once in a while."

I snuck a look at Calypso again. She was so obviously embarrassed that I began to feel sorry for her.

"The next thing I knew," Lady said, "Michael showed up at my office and offered the Mermaid's Lament as a token of his affection." She paused. "I wouldn't accept it of course."

She shifted her gaze to the sea goddess and her voice softened. "We've been friends too long, Calypso, for me not to help you find your property, since I know the thief." Her voice chilled again. "But one more attempt on my life or the lives of anyone in my employ and you'll get not my help, but my wrath."

I watched the two goddesses. There was clearly no love lost between them. Califia was only in this hunt because Calypso had threatened to flood the state if Calypso didn't get her necklace back. And, though she'd probably never admit it even to herself, I thought Lady felt a little guilty that it was her suitor who'd stolen the necklace. Calypso was still angry because she thought the *Pride of Zubris*, which had started Lady's empire, was her property, which Lady had stolen. And Calypso had put herself in the situation that allowed her pearls to be stolen and it embarrassed her. Yeah. There was a bit of history between these two.

My only concern at the moment was my continued breathing for a few more years.

"Can you guarantee our safety back to the mainland?" I asked the sea goddess.

Calypso seemed surprised that I'd spoken. I think she'd forgotten I was there. The sea goddess hadn't acknowledged

Edwin's presence at all. He stood behind us where the land sloped up at the back of the cove. He wasn't hidden and Edwin was pretty hard not to notice.

Calypso put her right hand on her chest. "You have my word that neither I nor anyone at my direction will harm you in anyway."

I looked for some sort of out in what she'd said, a 'gotcha' we wouldn't expect or guard against but couldn't find one.

Lady turned and called to Edwin. "Get the boat ready. We're leaving."

As Edwin sauntered toward the boat, Lady tuned a laser-gaze on Calypso. "Make your son stop these attempts. I will not tolerate any more attacks."

Calypso narrowed her eyes, but she nodded ever slightly. "You return my necklace, and we will call our debts even. I will relinquish my claim on *The Pride of Zubris* and you will not seek retribution for any of the attacks."

I tilted my head and regarded the sea goddess. Was she admitting she'd orchestrated the attacks, or was she protecting her son?

Lady nodded about as little as one could and still do it.

The sea goddess drew in a breath. "I will have a word with Saylor. If he is responsible for the water attacks, he will be punished."

Lady showed no sign she'd heard, but I was sure she had.

Edwin had managed to push the boat off the beach and into the water by himself. He held the bowline in one hand and used his free hand to turn the boat sideways, so Lady and I only had to get wet to our waists to reach a rope ladder thrown over the side.

Lady climbed on board first and took her place in the captain's chair. I went next and took my seat in behind where

Edwin would sit next to Lady. Edwin threw the line up on the bow and then made a standing jump to land next to the rope. The boat bobbed under his sudden weight. He walked up the long deck, stepped over the windscreen, and settled himself in the chair. I glanced back at the beach and saw Calypso's clenched jaw and narrowed eyes as Lady started the engines and we left Rippers Cove behind.

Lady waited until we were back on land to tell me what had angered her at Rippers cove.

"Just because I allow you to speak freely to me does not mean you may speak freely to all the godly," she said after grabbing my arm and holding me back as Edwin continued up the dock towards the parking lot. "For you to speak to Calypso like that, without asking my and her permission first, was highly inappropriate."

I felt my cheeks warm. It was like getting bawled out by the principal.

"I didn't know," I said.

"Did you pay no attention to how Edwin behaved? How he stood quietly away from Calypso and me? I expect you to be more aware, Shayna."

I was equally pissed about being berated over things I knew nothing about and embarrassed that I hadn't paid attention, hadn't realized there was a protocol.

"Now I know," I said.

"Yes," Lady said and strode off down the dock.

I followed, still angry and slightly ashamed. It wasn't an emotional mix I was used to. Neither Lady nor Edwin seemed to notice or to care that I rode all the way to the house in silence.

A really hot shower and a change of clothes later, I felt ready to be enticed from my room by the wafting scents of something delicious coming from the kitchen. I padded sock-footed down the hall, following my nose. My one pair of jeans was completely salt-stiffened, so I wore red-and-black plaid flannel pajama bottoms and a black t-shirt. My stomach rumbled and I realized I hadn't eaten since that morning.

Edwin was in the kitchen when I walked in, his back to me, humming under his breath as he lifted a spoon to his lips to taste what he was cooking. Without turning he said, "Have a chair. This will be done in a few minutes and there's more than enough for two."

Evidently Edwin wasn't holding my faux pas against me.

"What about Lady?" I said. "Does she not eat except for show, being a goddess and all."

Edwin turned to face me; the spoon still held in his hand. "She eats, sleeps, and probably does all the things regular folk do. She's gone out."

He took in my outfit. A bemused smile crossed his lips, but he made no comment.

I answered with a shrug and said, "That smells good."

He turned back and gave the pot a final stir. "It's cannelloni, quinoa, and kale soup. Hot, hearty, with plenty of protein. Perfect comfort food after a day like we had."

And vegetarian. Coincidence or consideration?

Edwin opened a drawer under the cook top and pulled out a large, silver ladle. He took two white porcelain bowls from a cupboard, spoons from another drawer (Asian style spoons, like tiny deep ladles themselves.) and filled both bowls with soup. He put one in front of me at the table and took a chair opposite with his own bowl.

I spooned up a swallow, blew on it to help it cool, and tasted. My eyes opened wide in surprise.

"This is beyond delicious."

Edwin grinned. "Cooking is only one of my many talents."

I chortled under my breath and tore into the soup. I knew I was hungry but hadn't realized I was ravenous.

I was more than halfway through my bowl when Edwin cleared his throat. I felt his eyes on me and looked up.

"Thanks for your help today," he said.

"You're welcome," I said but waved his thanks away with a flick of my hand. We'd all helped each other out there today.

I ate a few more spoonfuls of the delicious soup wondering if Edwin would mind being questioned by me. Some people were fine with it; others felt it as an invasion of privacy.

I set down my spoon.

"What are you, Edwin? You have some mad magic skills, but you don't feel like a wizard, witch, or mage to me."

He shrugged. "Demigod. Like Saylor."

I must have looked surprised or skeptical because he said, "There are lots of us around. The gods and goddesses are practically immortal. They get bored. One way to relieve the tedium is to seduce mortals."

Which explained Lady's comment about Michael Rawlings being an amusement, I thought.

Edwin smiled thinly. "The mortal women and the goddesses get pregnant often enough from these liaisons that there's no shortage of demi-gods in the world."

I was intrigued, which I thought must also show on my

face because Edwin smiled like he'd told this story a hundred times, but he'd indulge me.

"I'm named for my father—the east wind, which is one of the sun god's favorite guises. Mother is human."

"But Lady is a full-on goddess?"

Edwin nodded. "Califia is the child of the sun god, Ra—"

I held up my hand to stop him. "Ra?"

Edwin nodded again. "Like all the gods and goddesses, he's been called by a lot of names. Ra is the one he likes best. I think he misses the days when the Egyptians worshipped him. He doesn't get devotion like that today."

He spooned another bite of soup into his mouth and swallowed before he continued. "After Mom named me Edwin—as close to *east wind* as she could come without saddling me with a name that would bring me loads of grief as a kid—Dad told her a better name would have been Ray. That bastard is never satisfied with anything any human does."

I gave him a sympathetic smile. I'd had great parents, but a lot of my friends growing up hadn't. One needn't be a god or goddess to be an asshole.

"Califia," Edwin said, "is the daughter of Ra and the old goddess of California, who called herself Gaietta, little Gaia, after her mother, the earth goddess, who also calls herself Hutash, among other names. Which makes Califia my half-sister." He laughed. "Things get complicated in families like mine."

"Evidently," I said, my head slightly swimming with this new and slightly weird information.

He gestured toward my bowl. "You done. Do you want some more?"

"I'm good, thanks."

Edwin stood, gathered my dishes and his, and rinsed them

in the sink. He lifted the top off a cake plate and returned with a piece of homemade baklava for each of us.

"Gaia/Hutash has plenty of 'pure bred' kids with Silver Fox, who created the world," he said, sitting back at the table. "Full on gods and goddesses, not demis—halfs—like Saylor and me. Gaia gives each of her 'pure' children a piece of land for their kingdom. All the states have a god or goddess to look out for them. Each of the Canadian provinces has one, and each state in Mexico. Little countries, like they have in Europe get a god or goddess each. As boundaries change, wars often break out over who gets what under the new boundaries. The gods and goddesses aren't much different from human families in their squabbling."

We both turned back to nibbling on the baklava. It was scrumptious.

"Did you make this?" I asked.

He nodded. "Do you want another piece?"

I grinned. "Yes, please."

As long as Edwin seemed in a talkative mood, I thought I'd press for more information.

"Is the Mermaid's Lament magic?" I asked. "Saylor said it was."

"It is."

"Magic how?"

Edwin chuffed, blowing enough breath out to slightly flutter his lips.

"Lady and Calypso are immortal, or as immortal as they can be. So long as one person somewhere on earth worships the sea goddess, she's good. It's a little trickier for Lady since people these days tend not to worship the particular ground on which they live. But Gaia is still honored and worshipped, and she siphons some of that to her land-children, so they're good."

"But," I said, because I could hear that coming.

"People like Saylor and me, we're finite, which I'd guess is why Saylor wants the necklace. It gives the wearer immortality."

I gaped at him. "Immortality? Really?"

Edwin nodded.

I ran my hand through my hair. "No wonder Saylor wants it so badly." I paused, thinking. "Is it general knowledge what the pearls do? Does Michael Rawlings know? Or his sister?"

"No," Edwin said. "A lot of people know there's magic there and think they know what the necklace does, but the truth is a closely held secret. I can count the people who know the truth on one hand."

I regarded him. "Why tell me?"

He shrugged. "I don't know. It just seemed like I should." He hesitated. "It's probably better if neither Lady, or Calypso, or Saylor for that matter, know I told you. Like I said, a closely held secret."

"Of course," I said.

"Calypso is probably kicking herself that she told Saylor," he said. "She doesn't know I know and it's much better for you if neither Calypso nor Lady know you know."

"Protocol," I said.

He smiled thinly. "Got the lecture, did you? Lady can decide to stand on ceremony or not according to her whim. It can be hard to know what will set her off."

"So I learned," I said.

I wasn't surprised that Saylor had lied about what the necklace could do. Much better for him if I believed the necklace might be used for an evil purpose rather than knowing it grants immortality to the wearer. Much better that everyone hunting for it not know its true magic, lest the finder keep it for him or herself.

"Why try to kill us?" I said. "Wouldn't it be easier for Saylor if the necklace was recovered?"

"Only if he can get ahold of it before Calypso does. She guards that thing much more closely than she does any of her children. She keeps it 'just in case.' Each pearl is an individual part of the full spell, so the necklace only works intact."

Evidently, even immortals worried about death.

"I'm having a hard time picturing Saylor with a strand of pearls around his neck," I said, hoping to lighten the somber mood our conversation had brought.

Edwin chortled. "That's a lovely visual. He doesn't have to wear them the way they are now, though. He can refashion the necklace into a bracelet or even use them as buttons. As long as all the pearls are there and in order, the spell holds."

"So, the best thing we can do is find the necklace and make sure it winds up in Calypso's, not Saylor's hands."

"For Lady's sake, yeah," Edwin said. "Once those two quit their feuding, I don't really care who winds up with the Mermaid's Lament."

I took that in. Edwin's loyalty was to Lady. Nothing else mattered.

He stood and stretched. "It's late. I'm going to turn in. See you in the morning."

I stood and we walked out of the kitchen together, though he turned to the left and I turned right to reach my room. The sheets and comforter were every bit as luxurious as they'd been last night, but I couldn't sleep. I lay awake a long time thinking about goddesses, demigods, and a necklace that let its owner live forever.

14

On the morning I showered, used the toilet, and pulled on my salt-encrusted jeans—the only ones I had—and a new sea-foam green t-shirt—the color seemed appropriate. I padded barefoot down the hall towards the kitchen. The scents of onions and garlic sautéing drew me on like an irresistible force.

It struck me that I'd been staying at Lady's for only two days and—despite getting reprimanded yesterday for inappropriate behavior—felt comfortable enough to go to breakfast barefoot, assumed Edwin had made enough for three, and there was a place and a plate waiting for me at the table. I'd worn pajama bottoms down for a snack last night, but that had been just Edwin and me. This morning, I presumed Lady would be there.

She was. But in the kitchen, not the breakfast room, which surprised me. The kitchen table was covered with a white linen tablecloth that hadn't been there last night. The tablecloth had a waving line of orange California poppies embroidered around the edge. A nicety I suspected Lady insisted on—both the tablecloth and the poppies. I was happy to see there was a plate and silverware waiting for me.

"Good morning, Shayna," Lady said as friendly as ever.

Edwin looked up from his plate filled with eggs scrambled with onions, garlic, and mushrooms, as well as four pieces of sourdough toast. "Eggs are on the stove in the kitchen. Toast is warming in the oven. Take your plate."

"Good morning," I said and nodded my thanks to Edwin, took the empty plate, and helped myself to the eggs and toast.

Edwin saw me eyeing a half full pot of coffee on the blue-tiled counter.

"Mugs are in the middle cabinet," he said.

Between bites of really delicious eggs, I surreptitiously watched Lady and Edwin eat. I've seen a lot of 'out-of-the-ordinary' things, but I've never had breakfast with a goddess and a half-god before. Both ate with amazing gusto, forking a new bite into their mouths as quickly as they could get their hands to the plate for more and back to their mouths. You'd think neither of them had eaten for days.

When Lady slowed a bit, I said, "Do you have something specific for me to do this morning? A new lead to follow?"

Lady daintily wiped her lips with a cream-colored cloth napkin. "Find the Mermaid's Lament before Calypso covers my land with salt in a couple of days."

My face warmed. "Of course." I hesitated, then plunged ahead. "You have several hunters out looking. My specialty is recovery. If there's nothing pressing that only I can do—" I paused again. "I need to salvage my personal things from my house."

Lady regarded me for a moment. "Yes. Of course you do. Go."

"Thanks," I said. "I should be back by ten-thirty." Another thought struck me. "Or if you don't need me until later, I'd like to go and speak with Michael's other girlfriends."

Lady waved her hand idly. "There's no need for that. I've determined that they have nothing useful to add. Go. Tend to your possessions and come back. Saturday is coming quickly, Shayna. Do keep that in mind."

As if I'd forget—or she'd let me forget.

I moved my head a little to include both Lady and Edwin with my next sentence. "Thank you for breakfast." I paused. "If you normally eat meat with breakfast, or any meal, don't change because of me. I don't mind."

Lady regarded me with a non-committal gaze. Edwin shrugged. I shrugged, too, and

went back to my room for my purse and keys. Minutes later I was headed down the hill towards home.

It's about a thirty-minute drive without traffic from the top of Palos Verdes into Hermosa Beach. I had time to think as I wended my way down the hill and then turned to follow the coast. There was a lot to think about. Mostly, being the bottom-line person that I am, I thought about how to find and retrieve the Mermaid's Lament. Which could be tough since there was more I didn't know than I did know.

I didn't know where Lady's enthusiastic suitor, Michael Rawlings, was. I didn't know if he had the Mermaid's Lament with him, or if he'd handed the pearls off to someone, or hidden them someplace. I didn't know how much, if anything, Saylor knew about where the necklace might be. Or if Calypso knew, for that matter. Maybe she was playing Lady for reasons of her own. I had the sense those two had been trying to one-up one another for a long time.

I drove through Hermosa and turned up 19th Street having reached zero conclusions. I stopped at the front house where my landladies lived and knocked. No one seemed to be home.

I went around back to see what sort of shape my house was in today. The windows were open, but the front door was locked. Seemed pretty silly to me, but I supposed it just didn't set right with Darci and Bella, my landladies, to leave my house unlocked.

When I keyed the front door open and stepped inside, my heart sank. I loved my little house, and it was in tatters. I stood a moment, closed my eyes, and sighed. What was done was done. Now it was time to see what could be salvaged.

The overpowering stench of sewage was gone, thank God, replaced by a fainter, slightly stinky garbage scent. The big fans were still blowing. The carpet squelched under my feet.

My couch was definitely ruined. The fabric was stained where the water had soaked it. The cushion stuffing was still wet and had turned mushy. Stuffing dangled from the couch's bottom where the webbing had given up the struggle to hold water-soaked sponge in place.

The dining chair that had been lying on its back when I'd last been here stood upright now. I might be able to save it if I had the seat and back re-upholstered. The wooden legs were discolored from the water, but maybe they could be sanded down and re-stained.

The kitchen had fared better. The linoleum was wrecked, but the homeowner's insurance would cover that. My dishes, flatware, glasses, toaster, and blender were fine. The pots and pans under the cook top had gotten wet, but I could sterilize them clean and still use them.

In the bedroom, it was obvious the bed frame and maybe the box springs would have to be replaced. That burst pipe must have been carrying a lot of water to soak my things that far up.

Okay. New bed. Some new sheets. Blankets. Everything

could be replaced. It was only money.

I dreaded opening the bottom drawers of my dresser where I kept most of my keepsakes. Money couldn't replace those.

I hesitated, then made myself pull it open. A heavy lump formed in my chest. I pulled out the three photo albums, set them on top of the dresser and began leafing through them.

The albums were soaked, their covers twisted and warped by the water. The photographs of my parents, dogs we had while I was growing up, family vacations, my school pictures, photos of my friends—all destroyed. Photographs I'd long meant to scan into my computer but just hadn't quite gotten around to yet.

I knuckled my eyes, put the albums back and shut the drawer—the photos were beyond saving.

Mementos I'd kept on top of the dresser were ruined as well. A pheasant feather I'd found when the family had gone camping—now wet and bedraggled. A little straw purse my dad bought for me on a trip to Mexico shortly after my hair turned white—now lying on the floor, some of the straw broken and sprung so that it stuck out forlornly.

I backed up across the room until the backs of my legs touched my bed and crumpled on top of the quilt a friend had made for me. The fabric felt damp on my skin. The quilt was ruined, too.

I lay there for long, cold minutes and let the tears roll down my cheeks. *Lost. All that tangible proof of a life that was—gone now.*

After a while I knuckled my eyes and sat up.

Don't be stupid, Shay. Some precious things that can't be replaced are gone, but the memories are still there. You haven't lost any of those people. As long as you remember them, part of them lives on.

I made myself get up and walk to the closet. Might as well see how the things in there had fared.

All my shoes were ruined.

Fuck a bunch of shoes. Who cared about shoes?

My photographs. My little straw purse.

Damn.

I could tell myself any number of comforting things about memory and how those people and the things that reminded us of them remained in our heart—but the loss still hurt.

I sighed and pulled my blue, fit-in-the-overhead-bin suitcase from the high shelf it sat on and filled it with clothes. Underwear, a pair of jeans, seven or eight t-shirts, (I just grabbed. I didn't count.) two sets of pajamas, and a warm jacket. The shoes I was wearing were going to be it for a while.

From the bath, I grabbed my electric toothbrush, even though I had a manual one at Lady's, and my hairbrush.

I stood in the middle of the bedroom and looked around. It was going to be okay. Everything would dry out. I'd replace the couch, bed, shoes, clothing, and whatever else couldn't be salvaged. I still had a home. Just not one I could use at the moment.

A thought struck me. It was mighty convenient for Lady that my house had flooded right when it did. She had me at her house, at her beck and call now, didn't she?

My cell phone rang. I answered it with a weary hello.

"Hey Shay. It's Drew Miller. I have a lead on the necklace. Can you meet me at Scotty's in twenty minutes?"

Scotty's was a local eatery on the Strand, the walk street that buffered the multi-million-dollar beachfront homes and the actual beach from each other.

I told him I could.

15

One of the nice things about Scotty's was that it had its own parking lot. Beach parking is a bear since there are only so many places to put your car on the narrow streets and you're in competition with the eight million, nine hundred and thirty-seven other people who want that spot. On a nice day when beachgoers inundated the city, it was uncommon to have to park blocks and blocks from your destination. But with Scotty's you just drove on in and parked your car. It was a little bit of Hermosa heaven, that available place to put your car.

I walked inside the restaurant and looked around. I liked Scotty's, with its salmon-colored walls festooned with fishnets and its blue vinyl booths. I liked its faint burgers-and-fries coffeeshop scent and its view across the Strand to the beach beyond. It had a friendly, homey vibe. I needed a bit of homey vibe right about now.

I spotted Drew in a booth at the back of the restaurant next to a window looking onto the Strand. A tall man with short, very dark hair, wearing a flannel plaid shirt sat with his back to me. Drew saw me and gave a little wave. I walked over, past the other person, and sat next to Drew in the four-person booth.

From the front, the man looked like what you might expect from someone wearing a lumberjack shirt. I thought he might be good looking under the very bushy beard and long mustache, but it was only a guess. His eyes, in contrast to his dark hair, were a vivid purple. So, unless he, like me, had been touched by the woodland fairies, he was probably not completely human. Maybe not human at all.

"Shay," Andrew said, "this is my longtime friend, Bodie. Bodie, this is Shay."

Bodie extended a large hand that was attached to strong wrists that lead to arms with muscles I saw bulging under his long-sleeved shirt. I took his offered hand and shook it, a bit worried he might be one of those strong guys who liked to show it off with a crippling handshake. But he wasn't. He matched almost exactly the pressure and firmness I'd used.

"Hi," I said and gave him my best, open smile.

"Nice cloud hair," he said. His voice sounded like gravel running down a hillside.

"Thanks," I said using my best non-committal tone. I've had this hair for a long time. I've heard every remark that can be made about it. "Nice purple eyes."

Bodie smiled at the mention of his eye color, I thought, or maybe at my not-so-subtle method of pointing out I didn't think he was quite normal either. His purple eyes might put some people off, since it was so out of the norm. I thought they were fine.

The waitress, a young Latina, came to the table, her order book in one hand and a pencil in the other. This was another thing I liked about Scotty's—no high-tech punching in your order on a soulless tablet with a menu on it. Instead a real person came to your table and talked to you.

"Just coffee for me."

The waitress made a quick squiggle on her pad and went off to fetch a cup and a coffee pot.

Drew put down the piece of toast he'd been eating, took a swig of coffee, then nodded toward the other man. "Bodie and I were talking a little bit of shop, he's also in the recovery and salvage business, and he mentioned something I thought you'd find interesting."

I turned my attention to the violet-eyed man.

"Lady Califia and Calypso and her tribe aren't the only ones looking hard for the Mermaid's Lament," he said.

My heart stilled in my chest for a moment. There was something about his voice tone that made this sound like very bad news.

"Who? And why?"

Bodie lay his large hands on the table. "I know of at least two independent contractors—a shapeshifter, and a ghoul. I think the ghoul is working for a witch's coven. I think it got the job I turned down."

"Some witches approached you about finding the necklace?"

The large man nodded. "I declined. No good can come to anyone stupid enough to get between Califia and Calypso, no matter how special the prize."

I thought that was probably an accurate assessment.

"The witches and the shapeshifter must be aware of the pearls' value," I said, "to want it so badly."

Bodie's eyes sparkled with interest while the rest of his face hardly showed he'd heard what I'd said. My guess was that he didn't know himself what the necklace could do. I wondered if I'd just made a mistake alerting him to the special value of the pearls. Maybe he'd decide to look for it himself. Just what I needed.

"Well," Bodie drew the word out, "I'd imagine they think they know. There's a lot of conflicting information about those pearls."

"Like what?" I said.

"Like they give the power of flight. Or they make the wearer invisible. Or they let the wearer travel seamlessly between worlds."

His eyes held the glint of expectation. If he thought I was going to blurt out the actual power of the Mermaid's Lament, he was wrong.

"Which do you think is true?" I asked.

Bodie shrugged. His massive shoulders strained under the plaid shirt. "Take your pick. Any of them would make the pearls worth having."

And eternal life could make them worth even more.

The waitress returned and set a cup and spoon on the table in front of me. She filled the cup with coffee and asked, "Can I get you anything else?"

"No. Thanks," I said, and she moved off to help other patrons.

I poured cream into my coffee and stirred it idly, thinking. Lady had hired four experts in their fields to race for the Lament. Later, she'd hired me to—what? Join the race to find it or simply to retrieve it once it was located? I thought that maybe, at first, it might have been just for retrieval, but something had made her change her mind about me. Or maybe she was bored, and I looked like a shiny new toy.

At least two outside forces were also looking for the necklace—the witches and the shifter, if Body was right. Three if I counted Saylor as an outside, rogue force, which I was beginning to think he was.

Another question—why was Drew sharing this information with me? He could have kept it to himself and let me blunder into the other forces if I was unlucky.

I fixed my gaze on him. "Are you telling all of Lady's hunters about this, Drew?"

He hiked one shoulder. "Lady cut me loose this morning. Paid me off and sent me packing."

Surprised, I stared at him.

"I talked to Finn after," he continued. "Lady thanked them, paid them, and fired them this morning as well."

"What about—"

Drew cut me off. "She told Finn you would be the only hunter kept on the job."

"Did she tell him why?" I asked, totally thrown by this turn of events.

"No," he said. "No explanation, just the dismissal."

"Strange," I muttered to myself. And then said to Drew, "I'm sorry you're out of a job."

Drew waggled his fingers. "No worries. She's kind of a bitch to work for."

That was true enough.

"You must have impressed her," Bodie chimed in.

I regarded him a moment and then turned my attention back to Drew. "You could have told me about the ghouls and shapeshifter and being let go on the phone."

Bodie cleared his throat. "I wanted to meet you. Everyone's heard of you, but no one seems to actually have met you. I couldn't pass up the opportunity."

I had no idea what to say to that.

"Nice to meet you, too," I said, and felt like a ninny. My mind was stuck on those damn pearls. I addressed both men. "If you were to guess where the necklace was now, what would your guess be?"

Brodie shrugged. "I haven't thought about it. I turned the

job down; I'm not going to clutter my mind wondering about things that don't concern me."

I was about to say, "Fair enough," and press Drew for his guess when I caught sight of Saylor and four other men approaching the door into Scotty's from the Strand.

Scotty's had two doors, one that opened onto the Strand and one that lead to the parking lot. The doors were on opposite sides of the building.

I leaped to my feet. "We have to leave now. Go to the parking lot. Don't take the beachside door."

I threw a twenty-dollar bill on the table, which was the only denomination I had on me, having stopped at an ATM on my way to my house, and raced toward the door with Drew and Bodie right behind me.

In the parking lot, Drew grabbed my arm. "What did you see to send us jetting out of there?"

"Saylor. And friends. Four of them. More than we probably want to take on here, especially if we ever want to eat at Scotty's again."

Drew tilted his head slightly to the side. "If they were coming for a fight. Maybe they were hungry, or on their way somewhere and just passing by."

Had I overreacted? I didn't think so. I looked in the restaurant's windows and didn't see Saylor inside, but I couldn't see into the entire restaurant from where I stood. I walked over to look around the side of the building but didn't see Saylor and his companions on the Strand or on the beach.

But I'd seen Saylor's face when he'd caught sight of us through Scotty's window. It hadn't been friendly.

16

Probably I should have headed straight back up to Lady's and told her about seeing Saylor, but I didn't. I decided to swing by my house again before heading up the hill.

When I drove up, my landladies were standing in the street speaking with a man sitting in a white truck. The side of the truck read, in large red letters, *Jamison and Sons Plumbing*. I parked my car a few houses back and walked up to join them.

"We were just talking about you," Bella said.

Bella was the older of the two women, stretching comfortably into her late sixties. In contrast to Darci, who was forever changing the colors of her short-cropped hair, Bella had let hers go naturally steel gray and wore it in a smooth, shoulder-length bob. Both were wearing jeans and light pullover sweaters—Bella's in a pale turquoise and Darci's in a bright orange.

"Good that you're here, Shay." Darci indicated the man in the truck with a rise of her chin. "Mr. Jamison was under the house today and fixed your broken pipes. He still has a bit to do and will be coming back Monday."

"So, no running water until then?" I asked and wondered why he couldn't come back tomorrow. I really wanted back in my house.

Bella looked like the answer pained her. "No. I'm sorry."

Today was Thursday. I could stay at Lady's or at the residence hotel for a few nights if I had to.

Except if I didn't find the Mermaid's Lament and return it to Calypso by Saturday at dawn, if wasn't going to matter anyway. My house would be flooded again, with seawater.

If I were Michael Rawlings, where would I be? More to the point, who would I tell my location to?

Bella touched my arm. "You're a thousand miles away. Is everything all right?"

I pulled my thoughts back to the here and now.

"I came by the other day and got everything I needed," I said. "I just dropped by today to see how the drying out process was going and see how you two are."

Darci smiled. "We're fine. We've talked with our insurance man and all the structural repairs are covered."

The man in the truck cleared his throat. "If there's nothing else—"

"Not today," Bella said. "Thank you."

Mr. Jamison started the truck's engine and we moved from the street to the sidewalk.

"Will you come in for a while?" Darci asked. "It only takes a minute to put the kettle on."

I heard her words, but my mind had wandered elsewhere again.

"If you were in trouble, Darci, who would you turn to?"

Her forehead creased in concern. "You can always turn to us, Shay. No matter what you've done."

"Thanks." Darci and Bella were on my side no matter what, even when I didn't need the support. "I'm not asking for myself, though. Say you'd gotten yourself in a mess and people were after you, where would you go for help?"

Darci looked at her partner and smiled. That made sense, Darci and Bella had been together thirty years or there about. Of course, one would turn to the other.

"If you didn't have a partner?"

Darci seemed to be giving it some thought but Bella immediately said, "My brother in Florida."

Darci nodded. "I suppose my cousin, Nikolina. I'd do anything for her, and I think she'd do the same for me." Darci considered a moment more. "Yes. Definitely Nikki. Family sticks together."

"Right. Family," I said. "Thanks for the offer of tea, but I need to go see someone."

Darci kissed my cheek and I kissed hers to say good-bye.

"Be safe," Bella whispered as her lips brushed my cheek.

"Always," I said back, then headed off to see the witch.

I'm good with directions. Once I've been somewhere, I can usually get there again even if I have a different starting point. Getting from my house to Miranda Rawlings' had been easy. What wasn't going to be easy was getting past her wards.

I didn't know if she'd somehow sensed my coming or she'd put up protective wards after I'd left the first time, but they were there now and not little weakling wards either. I figured the best thing to do was to call her and ask her kindly to speak with me.

Yeah, like that was going to work.

I really didn't have another option. I dug my cell phone from my purse and then the piece of paper Drew had written her phone number on and given to me.

Of course, she might not even be home.

I punched in the number and listened to the rings. On the third ring, she picked up.

"I did not ask you to call," she said loudly and with heat in her voice. "I don't want to talk to you. Take me off your list. Now!"

I almost laughed. She hadn't recognized my number and thought I was a telemarketer.

"Miranda, it's Shay Greene. Please don't hang up. I have a proposition for you."

There was a long, long silence before she said, "What sort of proposition?"

"One that will be good for everyone involved," I said. "Are you at home?"

"No," she said, and I could hear in her voice that she was curious about whatever I might have in mind. "Where are you?"

"Near your house."

Another silence, this one shorter.

"I'll meet you at the foot of the Hermosa Pier in fifteen minutes," she said.

Ah. She wanted a public meeting place where neither of us was likely to set our magic on the other. Fine with me. But not the pier.

"Parking is hellacious this time of day. Meet me at Scotty's."

"Fine," she said and hung up.

For the second time today, I drove to Scotty's for a meeting.

I saw Miranda sitting at a window table when I pulled

into the parking lot. She was looking out, watching for me. I gave her a little wave and pulled into an empty spot.

She hadn't waved back, and she didn't smile when I sat down across from her. She didn't reply to my "Thanks for meeting me." The look in her eyes could have frozen the flames of hell.

Thank goodness the waitress came immediately. I ordered a coke and a side of fries. Miranda went for tea with lemon.

"You know that your brother is in a lot of trouble, right?" I said, after the waitress left to put in our order. The restaurant was still fairly full, even though the lunch rush was over and the dinner rush not yet begun. I kept my voice low.

"I know he went from being elated and proud of himself one day to being terrified for his life the next," she said coolly.

"You know what he stole."

Miranda fiddled with a sugar packet, her haughty demeanor gone.

"The necklace," she said finally. "That damn pearl necklace."

The waitress brought our drinks and my fries. I sipped my coke and ate a couple of fries before I continued.

"What if I could assure Michael that if he returns the necklace to me, I will guarantee no harm will come to him from Calypso or any of her agents?"

I'd thought she'd jump at the offer. She didn't. Miranda drank her tea while she considered what I'd said. I ate a couple more fries.

Finally, she put down her cup. "How can you guarantee his safety?"

Honestly, I had no idea how I was going to pull off what I'd just promised. What I said was, "I have my ways," and pitched my voice to make it sound like I did indeed have a secret method to make it happen. *Trust me*, my voice tone said.

Miranda drummed her fingernails on the tabletop and glanced around the room. If I didn't close the deal quickly, I was going to lose her.

"So, you do know where Michael is?" I asked.

She shook her head. "But I know how to get in touch with him."

Okay, that was progress.

"The best thing you can do for your brother is to tell him my offer," I said. "I'll meet him or his representative wherever he likes. All he has to do is get the necklace to me, and he can come home and have his regular life back."

Miranda was considering. I could see it on her face. She just needed a little push.

"He can't keep the necklace and he can't sell or trade it to anyone but Lady Califia or directly to Calypso. If he tries, they will hunt him down and make him wish he'd never heard of the Mermaid's Lament. You know how they are. You know that's true. But if he gives the pearls to me, his worries are over."

She broke then, everything that she'd been holding inside tumbling out at once. She kept her voice low and almost monotone. I had to strain to hear her.

"He told me what he'd done. He told me why. I screamed at him. Lady Califia! Of all people. Did he really think she'd be so impressed with his daring-do that she'd—what? Fall in love with him? Michael couldn't impress her with a shipload of pearls. She's Lady-fucking-Califia, the richest woman in America. What would she want with Michael Rawlings? She only let him hang around because she felt sorry for him. I told him that. He didn't take it too well, as you might imagine, but someone had to slap some reality into him, and I seemed to be the only one willing."

Her anger spent, she sighed and her shoulders visibly slumped.

"You love your brother a lot, don't you?" I said.

She nodded without looking at me. "Daddy tried to wedge us apart. He always said rivals were better for pushing each other to excellence than friends were. We were never rivals, Michael and I. It was always clear he'd get the business when Daddy retired or died. I always knew I had magic in me. I set about early on to develop that. I'm happier in the life I have than if I'd been expected to take over the business."

If this was all true, and it felt true, Miranda hadn't arranged her father's death. Was Drew simply mistaken, or had he told me that story to set me on the wrong foot? Mistaken, I decided.

There seemed to be a lot of *mistaken* and *wrong* in this job. Drew was wrong about Miranda, though she didn't do much to dispel her witch/bitch reputation. Bodie was wrong about what power the Mermaid's Lament really had. Michael was wrong that a trinket, no matter how valuable, would turn Lady's head and heart in his favor. And Saylor was probably seriously and dangerously wrong if he thought Calypso would let him keep the pearls if he got his hands on them first.

Miranda blew out a long, slow breath. "I love my brother with all my heart. I'd do anything for him."

"Then help him get out of the mess he's gotten himself into," I said. "Have him call me."

I reached into my purse, found a business card and handed it to her. The card had my name and, underneath it, the words Rescue and Recovery. My cell number was below that. She stared at it as if it were written in Martian.

"Okay." She put my card in her purse, stood, and walked out like a somnambulist. She'd get in touch with her brother, I was sure of that. Whether he'd call me was open to question. I'd worry about that later. The next thing on my agenda was to get Lady and Calypso to agree to what I'd promised.

17

Hermosa Beach and Palos Verdes weren't far apart as the crow flies, but to get to Lady's house I had to wend my way up the hill's long, narrow roads. It was a nice drive, sometimes offering glimpses of the ocean below, and with trees all around. I drove past little shopping centers, a private school for the children of the wealthy, houses that cost more than I'd make in my lifetime, and joggers and dog walkers on the raised paths, most wearing some sort of reflective covering to make them visible in the gathering gloom of nightfall. The drive gave me time to formulate my arguments for Lady and Calypso.

I turned up a narrow, crooked road and slowed on the dark, unlit street. I still had no idea why Palos Verdes didn't have streetlamps, especially for roads like this one—houseless, the twisting asphalt ribbon surrounded by trees, brush, and rolling hills. Lady and Edwin drove this road like it was a high-speed straightaway, but they'd been driving it for years and knew its idiosyncrasies. Not to mention that they could have powers and abilities I was still unaware of. I took the road slowly and carefully.

Something banged hard against the driver's side of my car. The car rocked from the blow. I yelped, my heart beating fast, and swung my head to look even as I struggled to keep the car on the road.

The ghoul had barely any skin stretched over its frame and little remained was scarred as if the thing had been burned head to toe, leaving a bald and puckered scalp. The bone structure said she'd been a woman in life. A very tall, strong woman.

I swerved the car first left then right then left again on the narrow road, trying to throw the ghoul off. She clung on as if her hands were superglued to the door handle.

The car windows were up, but the ghoul's stench of rot and putrefaction came right on through the glass, strong enough to make my eyes water.

I slammed on the brakes in another try at throwing the ghoul off my car. The thing grinned, a horrid, toothy smile beneath the hole where her nose should have been. She still had eyeballs in their sockets, and she glared at me with such scorn that I hit the gas again to get away from her lidless, staring eyes.

Not that it did any good. The ghoul still clung to the door. The crack of metal as the door was ripped off its hinges sent my heart racing even faster. From the corner of my eye, I watched the door fly away and land among the trees.

With the door gone, the ghoul stood with her feet on the edge of the carpeted interior. She stood fairly upright, with her arms stretched over the car's roof. I slammed on the brakes again and immediately accelerated, heading down the bumpy road at much too fast a speed to be safe.

The ghoul gimbaled her knees and rode the speeding car as nonchalantly as if it were a child's ride at the amusement park. She pulled one grotesque arm from the roof and reached her gnarled hand toward me. I leaned away as far as I could and still keep control of the car. She took the other arm off the roof, balancing herself somehow with just her legs and feet. The ghoul leaned her putrid head close to mine. I struggled not to gag.

"Do you have it?" the ghoul said through swollen bluish lips. "Give it to me."

I swerved the car again, a quick right to left. An intersection loomed in front of us. Cars streamed on the street perpendicular ahead. I'd been alone on this less-traveled road. I couldn't keep swerving and abruptly starting and stopping once I hit the main thoroughfare.

I swerved left. None of it meant a thing to the ghoul. She reached into the car with both hands, yanked me from my seat, and threw me over her bony shoulder like a sack of potatoes. The stench of her body was overwhelming. I pulled my head up in a desperate try for fresh air, and saw my car jump the curb and hit a tree. At least it stopped there and didn't roll down into the main road or over the cliff.

I bounced against the ghoul's wretched flesh as she ran into the trees across from where my car had crashed. The ground was uneven, making each bounce harder and more jarring than it would have been if the ghoul had been running on the flat. I tried to think of a way to force her to trip over a root or stumble on a gopher hole, but the ghoul never misstepped. Even if she fell, could I outrun the thing? I wasn't sure. The dead woman was damn fast.

The ghoul came to a hard stop. I rose up in the air and I thought she was going to let me be flung backward onto the ground, but she caught me, flipped me around, and hugged me to her chest.

"Do you have it?" the ghoul said, the same words she'd used before.

"I don't have it," I managed to say. The ghoul's hug was crushing my lungs. "But I know where it is."

She loosened her hold and let me slide over her nasty flesh to the ground. I stepped back, worried the ghoul would see even a step as an attempt to run and grab me again. She didn't seem to think that. At least she didn't reach for me or tell me to stop. If she could tell me to stop. Maybe those two sentences were all she could manage. But she'd understood what I'd said. I was sure of that.

"The necklace is—" I said.

Where? What could I tell her? I couldn't lead her to Lady's or to my house, or to anywhere people might be.

The ghoul's lips drew back from her teeth in what I thought might be a smile.

"You think I'm stupid because I'm a ghoul," she said. "Right now, you have no more idea where the Mermaid's Lament is than I do."

"Well," I said, shaking off my stunned surprise, "if you thought that, why ask if I have it? And, by the way, why pretend you had about two sentences in your arsenal and nothing more?"

The ghoul stretched her mouth in a lazy, grotesque smile. "It serves our purpose to have others regard us as crazed mercenaries or mere eaters of the dead, only good for clean-up and other 'disreputable' jobs."

I took that in and added ghouls to the list of very smart adversaries to watch out for.

"If you were aware I didn't know where the pearls are, why go to all that effort to get me here? My car is smashed—evidently for no good reason. You could have just waved me over or something."

The ghoul sighed and shrugged one shoulder. "A ghoul

needs a little excitement once in a while." She grinned. "It was a good workout. I need to keep in shape."

With a different workout partner next time. Thanks so much.

"Again, why chase me down if you knew I didn't have the necklace?"

"Because I don't want my employer to have it," the ghoul said.

That took me aback. "Why?"

"Because she's a selfish asshole and will use the Mermaid's Lament's power only to her own ends. Besides, it isn't hers. It should go back to the rightful owner."

She, the ghoul said. Maybe Bodie had been right and the ghoul was working for the coven Miranda was involved with, which I knew from Lady was all female. Or not. Could be a witch from a different coven easily enough.

"Your boss is a witch?" I asked to clarify things.

"Mmmm," the ghoul noised, adding, "No one you know."

So not Miranda, presuming the ghoul knew I had met Miranda. That didn't rule out others in her coven though.

"My employer is trying to return the necklace to its owner," I said.

"Yes, the estimable Lady Califia. If she really does want to return them."

I wasn't going to rise to that bait. "She does. It's to her advantage for the pearls to go back where they belong."

The ghoul turned and looked out into the trees. "I have some information that will help you." She turned back and gave me another one of her unnatural grins. "Think of me as a silent whistle-blower. No one will ever know how you discovered this information."

"No one will."

The ghoul seemed to draw in a deep breath. I wasn't sure if ghouls actually breathed or not.

"Miranda Rawlings has them," the ghoul said. "Her brother gave them to her before he, um, disappeared."

I thought about that. I'd already talked to Miranda twice, and yes, she'd been defensive, but I didn't think she had the necklace. Her anger at and concern for her brother were genuine, I thought. If she had the Mermaid's Lament, I felt sure she would have handed it over, or at least bargained with it, to keep her brother safe.

"Do you know where Michael Rawlings is?" I asked.

The ghoul shook her head. "No clue." She leaned toward me. I tried not to gag on her smell. "Do *you* know where he is?"

"I don't."

"Would you tell me if you did?"

"Maybe," I said. "It would depend on circumstances and if you had something useful to trade."

She straightened up. "I see what I've heard about you is true."

It kind of creeped me out that people seemed to have heard things about me—people I didn't know. People I didn't even know existed. I thought I'd kept a low profile. Evidently not. "What did you hear? And from whom?"

The ghoul only grinned again and shrugged one shoulder.

We stood without talking long enough that I felt she had something more she wanted to say. If not, why stay around?

"Who are you working for?" I asked to get us talking again. "A witch. What coven?"

The ghoul bared her teeth and laughed. "A ghoul doesn't kiss and tell. Not if she wants to keep working."

She went quiet again. I waited. She looked around the woods slowly, then shrugged. Without another word, the ghoul turned and ran through the trees away from the road. She was blazing fast. There was no way I could chase her, and I wasn't sure there was much of a reason to.

I walked back down the hill, picking my way through the trees and undergrowth to the road and my car. The front right fender was smashed in enough that the tires wouldn't turn freely. I glanced underneath and saw an axle was broken. This car wasn't going anywhere without help from a tow truck.

The left door was gone, but fortunately my purse with my phone in it hadn't flown out into the brush. I grabbed my purse, pulled my phone out of the little front pocket where it lives, and hoped I wasn't too far up the hill for reception. The phone showed three bars. It was my lucky day.

I rang up the towing service my insurance offers and leaned against my poor smashed Clarity to wait for the driver's arrival. Good thing I'd known the name of the little road I was on. Trying to describe where I was would have been hard to impossible.

That taken care of, my brain switched back to wondering why the ghoul had told me what she had. Did she really think Miranda Rawlings had the Mermaid's Lament, or was I getting too close to figuring out who really had it or where it was hidden and the ghoul wanted to slow me down with a false lead? Did the ghoul know I'd just come from talking to Miranda? Could she know I'd promised Miranda safety for Michael if the necklace was returned? How could the ghoul know that? Could the ghoul be working for Miranda, who really did have the pearls, but wanted me to think she didn't?

Thank goodness the tow truck showed up before I twisted my brain into a knot. The driver was a guy about my age who seemed to like his job, judging by how he hummed happily under his breath while hitching up my car. We drove together to a repair shop I knew of in San Pedro because I'd gone to high school with the owner's daughter. Those old school friendships come in handy later in life.

I got an estimate for the repairs, left my car in capable hands, and ordered an Uber to take me to Lady's.

The moon was well up by the time I made it to the house. Edwin must have seen or heard me arrive. He came out the front door and stood on the porch.

I tipped the driver with cash and watched him back up and drive off.

"What happened to your car?" Edwin said as I walked toward him.

I waved the question away. "Is Lady here?"

He shook his head. "Not back from the office yet. She phoned earlier to say she'd be a late. Why? Did you learn something?" He narrowed his eyes. "So, about your car."

"It's a bit of a story," I said.

"Hmm," he said. "Does it need tea and a sandwich?"

I smiled thinly. "I believe it does. Yes."

I followed him into the house and down the hall to the kitchen.

Lady's kitchen is a massive thing with a fifteen-foot high ceiling, black and white tiles on the floor, white subway tiles on the walls, restaurant-quality appliances, and an eight-person oak table. Four couples could waltz in that kitchen and not bump into the furniture or each other.

I sat down at the table.

Edwin put on the electric kettle and busied himself making sandwiches from the egg salad he'd made earlier. He spread the concoction on thick slabs of homemade wheat bread, plated them, and brought one to me and set down one for himself at a place across the table from where I sat. The kettle clicked off and Edwin walked back to where it sat on the counter.

"Can I ask you something?" I said as Edwin was pouring boiling water over a tea ball stuffed with hibiscus tea. I knew it was hibiscus from the delicate scent.

He looked at me over his shoulder. "Sure."

"You're a demigod, right?"

He walked the teapot and two cups over to the table and sat down.

"Right."

"So why have you chosen to be Lady's factotum? Shouldn't you be off doing more demigod sorts of things?"

"Like what?" he said as he filled my cup with sweet-smelling tea. "What do you think demigods should do with their time?"

He had me there. I had no idea what I though demigods should do all day. A week ago, the question never would have entered my mind.

"I don't know. Watch over something, I guess."

He chuckled to himself. "I do. I watch over Lady, this house, the garden. I help out wherever and however I can."

"Are you happy doing that?"

He drew in a breath and sighed it out. "I studied to be a veterinarian. I love animals. But when I got my degree, Dad showed up and said I couldn't do that. Evidently part of the demigod thing is having extra special abilities. In my case, healing. Dad said I'd be too good at my job and that would draw attention. The gods, goddesses, and the slew of us demigods around are supposed to keep a low profile, just like you magicals don't go around announcing yourself to the everyday folks." He grinned at me. "Though with that hair, people might suspect something."

"My hair is right in fashion," I said.

"Now," he said, "but not when you were growing up, and probably not five years from now either."

I squirmed a little. My hair was a touchy subject. Growing up, I'd taken plenty of ribbings and lots of name calling for something I had no control over.

"A ghoul attacked me tonight," I said to change the subject. "Wrecked my car."

He leaned forward, a worried look on his face. "What happened?"

I told him the whole story of my day, starting with my visit to Miranda, the rash promise I'd made to her, the ghoul ripping the door off my car, and what she'd said to me.

"What's your feeling?" he asked when I'd finished.

"I'm not sure," I said. "Miranda seemed pretty interested in her brother getting a free pass from Lady and Calypso if he returned the necklace. I didn't get the sense that she had it, but maybe she's a good actor. Or it could be the ghoul is misinformed. Or a good liar."

"Do you want to go see Miranda again?" he asked. "I'll drive."

"Can't hurt," I said. "Too late tonight, but first thing in the morning might shake her up enough that she'll spill something important."

A thought struck me. "I know Lady has the power to compel people to do what she wants. What about you? Can you compel people to do your bidding? Could you get the truth out of Miranda?"

Edwin shook his head. "I'm a fighter and a healer—a weird enough combination as it is. Add in compulsion and, I don't know, it would be overload, I think."

"So, no."

He turned his hands palms up. "Sorry."

18

Miranda was less than pleased to see me standing at her door again, especially since it was 6 a.m. That I had big, strong, no nonsense-looking Edwin with me didn't help either.

She opened her front door the very least she could and peeked out.

"No grass growing under your feet." Miranda scowled but opened the door all the way. "I've spoken to Michael. You might as well come in."

Miranda had cleaned up the shattered pottery and glass. She'd put her unbroken knick-knacks and photographs back up. The clear shape of where the big mirror had hung on the wall caught my eye, the paint darker where the mirror had protected the wall from the bleaching action of sunlight.

Miranda saw where my gaze had gone and scowled again.

"You've spoken to Michael," I said to change the subject before her anger worked itself all the way up.

She dropped her eyes from the spot on the wall and shifted her gaze to me. "I know where he is."

"Where?"

She crossed her arms over her chest. "It's not that easy. I know where he is, but he can't leave, and you can't get in."

I felt Edwin fidget next to me. Nervous? Impatient? Annoyed? It was hard to tell with him sometimes.

"Why can't he leave?" I asked.

Miranda's face grew dark. "Because some witches have him under a curse."

Realization hit me like a stone dropped on my head. "Your coven, Miranda. Who you told about the necklace and what you think it can do. Which got your brother kidnapped and cursed. You left the coven in protest, but as a favor, they still let you talk to him."

Miranda shook her head angrily. "That's exactly what happened. Damn bitches. Betrayed by my own coven-sisters."

I stared at her. "Why would you tell them about the necklace and that your brother had it? Seems pretty stupid."

She sighed. "I was trying to protect him from Calypso. She has a temper. A really bad temper."

The kind of temper that made Calypso threaten to flood half a state to get her pearls back. I couldn't blame Miranda from wanting to protect her brother from the sea goddess.

Still, something didn't feel right about her story. Then I had it. "Michael doesn't have the necklace with him. If he did, there wouldn't be a need for the witches to hold him captive."

"You have it," Edwin said, glaring at Miranda. "Or know where it is."

Miranda's neck and face colored. "All right. Yes. I know where it is. But it's cursed as well. By me. And nothing will make me remove my curse except you freeing Michael from those witches. Return my brother unharmed and I'll take you to the necklace and remove the curse I've put on it."

Edwin regarded her evenly. "What does your curse do?"

Miranda laughed. "Dissolves the string that holds the pearls." She laughed again. "I know how the necklace works. I know the pearls have to be in a certain order. The only way you'll get them back intact is if you save my brother."

"Miranda," I said. "Why not just give the Mermaid's Lament to your coven in exchange for your brother?"

"Calypso," she scoffed. "The sea bitch finds out I gave her precious Mermaid's Lament to my witch-sisters and I'm completely and utterly fucked. She'd come after me and there would be nothing I could do to protect myself. She'd probably go after Michael, too, in that case."

I turned to Edwin so Miranda couldn't see my face and winked at him. "Calypso isn't concerned about any power the pearls have. Why would she be? She's a goddess. I say we get Miranda here to tell us where they are—pain is useful for that—and just go get them. They can be restrung in any order, as far as Calypso cares."

"True," Edwin said at the same moment Miranda cried, "No!"

"No?" I said, turning back to Miranda.

All her anger and haughtiness had drained away. "Please. Save my brother. My sisters—my former sisters in the coven—are running out of patience with him. He's refused, so far, to tell them I know where the Mermaid's Lament is, but I think they're hurting him. They only let me talk to him because I said I'd try to get him to say where the necklace was. They weren't happy when our conversation didn't contain that information. They weren't happy he told me where he was either. They'll probably move him. You need to go now."

I gave a slight shrug. "Tell us where he is, and we'll do our best."

Miranda hesitated. Why hesitate now when we've agreed to do what she's asked?

She turned and disappeared into another room. Edwin and I looked at each other, both of us with our eyebrows raised in question and neither of us with answers.

"You can leave me here," I said, keeping my voice low. "I'll Uber to wherever Michael is."

He kept his voice just as low. "I could use a good adventure, if you don't mind company."

"The day I interviewed for this job," I said instead of answering, "there was a curse breaker also interviewing. Could you get her name and number from Lady?"

He nodded. "Sure. If you take me along to the witches."

I closed my eyes, thinking. Edwin had been pretty spectacular fighting the kraken. He didn't seem the sort of fool who'd get in my way with the witches. I was going to have to bring the curse-breaker anyway, so why not two people?

"Yeah. Okay. You can come along but follow my lead."

Edwin chuckled under his breath. "Whatever you say, ma'am."

I sent him a dark glare.

Miranda reappeared and handed me a piece of paper. I glanced down. She'd given me not an address, but a map. And not a very good one at that.

"What's this?" I asked.

"There's a coven safehouse

"I'll do my best. You have the Mermaid's Lament here when I return."

Miranda nodded. "Bring Michael. You really need to hurry."

Outside I said, "How much of what she said do you believe?"

Edwin shrugged. "Remember I told you I'd inherited

healing ability from my father? Along with that came the ability to sense people's pain. She's in agony worrying over her brother. I think the witches have him. She absolutely believes her brother is in great danger."

"So, she's unlikely to send us on a wild goose chase."

"Right," Edwin said.

I glanced down at the map in my hand again.

"Okay," I said. "Let's go see the witches, but we need to get the curse-breaker first," I said.

"Right," he said again.

Edwin pulled his phone from his pocket and punched up a number from his favorites list. The other person, Lady I assumed, answered and Edwin rattled off in a language that not only didn't I understand but that I didn't come close to recognizing.

He ended the call and started punching in an address on his mapping app. He caught me glancing at him.

"The curse-breaker is named Norena—her friends call her Nola—and she lives in Culver City," he said. "I have her address."

I nodded. "What language were you speaking with Lady?"

"The language of the gods. Even we demis learn it as children. It's structured differently than English and is good for getting ideas across quickly."

I took that in, my mind churning with plans, lining up all the dominos so they'd fall the way I wanted. "You didn't by any chance mention to her that I'd promised a free pass for Michael if the pearls were returned?"

Edwin shook his head. "I told her the witches have him. That they've placed a curse on him—which is why she couldn't feel him even though he was still in her State. That you're planning a rescue, hence the need for Nola. It's up to you to tell her the rest."

I bit my bottom lip, thinking. "Okay. Is Lady at home?

Edwin nodded.

"Good," I said. "Back to the house first. Then on to the curse-breaker."

Edwin raised his eyebrows.

"What?" I said.

"Nothing," he said.

"You don't think Lady will agree to the pardon?"

"Lady might," Edwin said. "But there's still Calypso."

Calypso had to agree, that was all there was to it.

"I'll cross that watery bridge when I come to it," I said.

19

Lady wasn't in the house when Edwin and I arrived. We spotted her through the kitchen window, outback, kneeling among a patch of purple flowers on a plant with thick, silvery leaves.

Edwin said, "It's better if you talk to her alone."

"Why is that?"

"She's funny that way," he said. "Take my word for it."

"Okay," I said, drew in a breath, and went out the back door and down a path covered in gray and black gravel to the garden. Cold tendrils of nerves wriggled in my chest. Lady was unpredictable. I'd made a deal in her name and had no idea what I'd do if she didn't agree.

She looked up from her gardening when I reached her.

"California Scorpionweed," she said, naming the ridge-leafed plant. "Lovely purple flower, isn't it? Honeybees love it."

Lady seemed very calm and in a good mood for a goddess who could soon see the land she was responsible for flooded with saltwater if Calypso didn't get her necklace back. Evidently, she had more faith in me than I did at the moment.

I stood silent, wondering how to broach pardoning Michael for the theft.

"When Edwin told you about the curse on Michael," I said. "There's more to it than the curse the witches have laid on him. Miranda has cursed the Mermaid's Lament itself. She offers a trade. You and Calypso promise no harm will come to Michael and she'll uncurse the necklace and have it returned."

Lady pulled to her feet and put her hands on her hips, her elbows jutting to the sides. "Miranda Rawlings will not blackmail me into anything. Fetch the curse-breaker. She can uncurse the Mermaid's Lament as easily as she can break the spell on Michael."

Shit.

I cleared my throat. "Maybe. But why chance it? More to the point, why chance Miranda refusing to say where the Mermaid's Lament is hidden or taking a hammer to the pearls when the easier thing to do is simply let Michael's foolishness be forgotten?"

Lady's voice, already cold, turned to ice. "I will not be blackmailed. Especially not by that witch. It's probably her coven that kidnapped Michael in the first place."

"It is," I said.

"Ah," Lady said, her voice returning to normal. "The whole thing is likely a trick then. There's probably no curse on Michael at all. I'll make my promise and she'll keep the necklace until it's too late." She bent down and yanked a weed from the dirt. "No. I will not have it."

I tried another approach. "Edwin says he feels Miranda is sincerely concerned for her brother."

"Does he?" she said, her voice reasonable again.

"I agree with Edwin."

Lady cut more purple scorpionweed flowers and seemed

to be considering my words. She had a bunch big enough for a large vase but kept snipping.

I offered her an out. "Easy enough to make your promise conditional. You'll pardon Michael only if the Mermaid's Lament is in Calypso's hands, in perfect condition, by Saturday at dawn. Which, I'm sure I don't need to remind you, is tomorrow. We're running out of time."

She stopped snipping and gave me a level gaze.

"Fine," she said.

A bit of the tension that had stiffened my shoulders drained away. "Thank you. You've made a good decision." There was just one matter remaining. "Will Calypso also agree?"

Lady shrugged. "You'll have to ask her."

How was I going to do that? I couldn't simply go to the water's edge on some random beach and wait for Calypso to show up.

Lady gathered up the cut flowers and started toward the house. She glanced over her shoulder at me.

"You'd better hurry, Shayna, if you want to accompany me to speak with the sea goddess."

I'd thought we might have to take the speedboat to Catalina again, but Edwin drove us down the hill to Malaga Cove. We parked on the street high above the sand and water.

During the drive, Lady had said, "Part of the reason I hired you, Shayna, was your control over the elements. Good job on the way to Catalina, by the way. I'd imagine it's difficult to control a body of water as large as the ocean."

I'd nodded slightly in admission. I'd never tried to control something that large before. It had been hard, but I'd pulled it off. Which, I'd realized, left an opening for Lady to request more control over the elements.

"There will probably be people on the beach," she said. "Perhaps you could send a very cold wind to encourage them to leave."

It hadn't been a request.

Not that it mattered. I rented myself out, complete with whatever talents and resources I possessed. Lady wasn't the first employer who'd wanted use of every item in my bag of tricks.

From the street, looking down on the rocky beach and water, I spotted a couple with their dog and another couple with two children. It shouldn't be hard to get them to leave.

I summoned up a very cold and raucous wind and sent it roaring around the cove. What little sand was there blew with the wind, pelting the visitors. I felt sorry about that, but wind did what wind did. I couldn't send a harsh wind but stop the sand from blowing.

Or maybe I could. I'd controlled wind and water on the trip to Catalina. I'd experiment later. Now the only thing that mattered was getting Calypso to agree with pardoning Michael.

We watched as the people who'd brought jackets hastily put them on. The couple with the dog was first up the long path up the cliff back to the street. They nodded at us as they headed toward their car. The couple with the children took longer to gather up their things and make it back to the street. They passed us with hardly a glance, the parents herding their kids to the car.

I calmed the wind. We headed down the cliff and across the rocky beach to the water.

Edwin and I stopped at the water's edge, but Lady waded right in. When she was knee deep, Lady bent and wiggled her hands in the water, stirring up a little splash. Some sort of silvery-gray fish, about the length of my fingertips to my elbow, popped its head out of the water and then dove back under. Lady hunkered down until she was neck deep in the water, then spoke in a language I couldn't understand, though it didn't seem to be the same language Edwin had used with her earlier. The cadence was different, and this was much more guttural.

Edwin said, "She's asking the fish to tell Calypso that Lady needs to speak with her now—it's urgent."

I'd pretty much figured that out.

Lady waded back onto the beach with us, seemingly oblivious, or not bothered, that her clothes were soaked. I summoned up a gentle, warm breeze to help her dry.

She inclined her head in acknowledgement. "Thank you, Shayna."

I shrugged and then pointed out to sea where a sudden wake had appeared. Calypso shot out of the water like a flying fish and landed feet first on the beach near us. Water dripped from her long hair and glistened on her naked body.

I saw in her face that being summoned this way irritated her. She stood with her legs apart, one hand on her hip, her eyes hard and fixed on Lady.

"What is so important that I should drop everything and come racing over to talk to you?" she demanded.

"If you want your necklace back," Lady said, evidently unimpressed with Calypso's black mood, "put your pout away and listen to Shayna."

The sea goddess rolled her eyes but deigned to give me her attention.

I cleared my throat. "I've been to see Michael's sister, Miranda. She's willing to tell us where Michael is, but she wants a guarantee from you and Lady that if he returns the necklace, neither of you or any of your agents will harm him. Ever."

It seemed better for me to phrase this as a demand from Miranda rather than a rash promise I'd made. Yeah, I fudge things on occasion.

Calypso glared at me. She drew in a deep, deep breath and let it out slowly and noisily.

"I will agree if he one, returns my necklace in perfect condition and two, never steps foot into my waters nor rides over them in a boat, ship, kayak, or other conveyance, nor flies over them in a plane."

I ran my hands over my hair. Why did the goddesses have to make everything so damn hard?

"He can't make that or any other promise until we rescue him from the curse that's keeping him wherever he is now," I said.

Calypso snorted. "You don't know where he is? Or where my necklace is?"

"I know where he is," I said, which was vaguely true. I had a map. "He doesn't have the Mermaid's Lament. Miranda knows where it is. She'll tell us when she has your promise."

"And I," Calypso said, "will make no promise until he has made his and I have the necklace."

I sent my gaze toward the sky, but no solutions were written there.

"You're putting us at an impasse," I said. "If you want your pearls, you need to make this small compromise and promise. Really, once the Mermaid's Lament is returned, what do you care if Michael Rawlings flies over the ocean on his way somewhere else?"

"I care," Calypso said slowly, "because mortals trespassing into my domain, mortals stealing my treasures, must be punished. He's fortunate I'm not asking for more. And worse."

Lady tsked loudly. "You always have to make a big show of things. Always want to be the center of attention. Give it a rest, Calypso. Say yes and let's move on with this."

"I will not," Calypso said. "Additionally, I want a personal apology from Michael Rawlings. He will face me and say he is sorry for what he's done."

Lady sighed noisily. "If you won't agree, that's your choice, but understand that my obligation to you is fulfilled and you will not hold me to your threat if the necklace isn't returned by tomorrow at dawn. If you won't promise, then Michael Rawlings can sell the Mermaid's Lament to the highest bidder for all I care—and you will not hold me to blame for anything that happens."

Calypso glowered at Lady. Lady glowered back. The air seemed to crackle with the electricity of their standoff. The sea roiled and waves crashed against the shore. I wouldn't have been terribly surprised if the small rocks we stood on suddenly burst into flames.

"Fine," Calypso spat. She turned to me. "You have my word. But if the Mermaid's Lament is not in my hands by dawn, I am relieved of my promise."

20

*C*alypso dove back into the sea. We land creatures went back to Lady's where she called Nola, the curse-breaker. I could only hear one side of the conversation, but I suspected Nola was asking some questions that Lady didn't feel like answering, judging from the dark cloud Lady's expression was taking.

"I would consider it a favor if you would meet with Shayna and help her any way you can," Lady said in the persuasive tone I recognized from the day of my interview. "She and my personal representative will pick you up in under an hour."

So, it was back into Edwin's SUV for the forty-five-minute ride down the hill and through town to pick up the 405 Freeway to Culver City.

Edwin had already put Nola's address in his phone for directions. Once we'd left the freeway, it didn't take more than ten minutes or so to find her house.

The curse-breaker lived on a cul-de-sac in a cute, blue shiplap-sided bungalow. I'd guess the house had originally been built in the early 1900s but had been well restored. We found a place to park on the street and walked up a flat-stone path to reach the bright red front door. Evidently Nola didn't feel a need to keep a low profile among her neighbors.

She opened the door almost as soon as we knocked and invited Edwin and me in. She was as short and thin as I remembered her. She must be a 'fun with hair' person because what had been short, spiky brown hair when I'd met her was now a pink fauxhawk. She made me feel not so odd with my hair, but I was almost a decade older than her. Maybe too old to be running around with unnaturally colored hair, despite the various colors my sixty-something landlady sported. Nola wore a simple black sheath dress, belted at her waist, over black leggings. Her feet were encased in serious looking Doc Martin ankle boots.

Nope. Nola felt no need at all to show a subdued façade to the world.

"I remember you from the interview," she said, gesturing toward a denim-colored couch in silent invitation for us to sit. "I wondered who had gotten the job—you or the other one who'd been selected along with me. That really tall woman dressed in leather."

There was no animosity in her tone, no hint that she resented being asked to help the person who'd landed a job she'd wanted. I decided direct to the problem at hand was best.

"It's a bit of a story as to why we're here," I began.

"You need to break a curse, according to Lady Califia," Nola cut in. She still stood. She'd centered herself between Edwin and me as though she wasn't sure which of us to give her attention to. "Person or thing?"

"Person," I said. "His name is—"

Nola cut me off again with a wave of her hand. "Don't tell me. It's better if I don't know the person's name or how they came to be cursed. Information colors things for me. I'm better off reading the curse cold."

"Okay," I said slowly. "Do you want to know where we're going to try to break the curse?"

Nola smiled. "Surprise me."

There was no way to plug the exact location of the witches into the GPS, but Edwin had looked at the map Miranda had drawn and was fairly certain how to get there from where we were.

We drove almost the same route back as we'd taken to pick up Nola. It was a long ride with people who didn't have much to say to each other and none of whom seemed to be proficient in the art of small talk. The silence was only broken when Nola said, "So this job is a one-off?" She paused. "Could it lead to more work for Lady?"

Edwin glanced at her sitting in the back seat. "It's a one-off for now, but Lady is known to be generous and she employs a lot of people."

How cagey, Edwin, I thought. Dangle the prize without ever actually offering it. I held my breath just a little, hoping Nola hadn't picked up to how noncommittal he'd been. She fell back quiet, so either she hadn't, or she'd decided to ignore it.

The second time the silence was broken was when we began climbing back up into Palos Verdes and Edwin started giving me directions based on the map. The map had only three roads named on it—Crest Road, Hawthorne Boulevard, and Palos Verdes Drive South. All the other streets were nameless wavy lines. Edwin knew the area though, and all those wiggly lines seemed to make sense to him, given the confidence with which he drove and the roads he chose to turn on.

We parked on Pacifica Drive and took a small, nameless trail that met up with the larger McBride Trail. I knew this was McBride because I read the signs. In front of us lay green rolling hills dotted with small copses of trees and deep canyons that stretched a long, long ways.

"Where are we?" I asked Edwin. I turned to Nola. "Is it a problem if you know the name of the place."

Nola, who was staring out over the open land stretching out before us, shook her head. "Are we going in there? Because I'm not much of a hiker."

Neither was I, for that matter.

"What is this place?" I said again to Edwin.

"Filiorum Reserve," Edwin said, "And according to the map, it is exactly where we are going. The place Michael is being kept is somewhere in there." He moved his hand to indicate the totality of the land. Acres and acres of scrub and tree dotted hills.

My heart sank. It was a lot of land to cover.

"How big is this reserve?" I said.

"Not quite two hundred acres," he said.

Shit. "Do many people hike here?"

Edwin nodded. "Some. There are probably people hiking here every day, though not hordes."

I bit my lip, thinking. We were going to have to find this hidden place—it would likely have to be hidden or nearly inaccessible for people not to have stumbled across the witches and Michael by now, if people hiked here every day —with nothing more than vaguely drawn lines on a map to guide us. A map that may or may not be accurate.

I believed Miranda was sincere in wanting her brother rescued, but she only had Michael's word that he was being held captive and where. For all I knew, Michael and the witches could be in it together—get Miranda riled up enough that she'd bring them the pearls. If that were the case, they were going to be mighty unhappy when the three of us showed up instead. I hoped we weren't going to have to kidnap Michael from his so-called abductors. Things would be complicated enough if Michael was only their prisoner and not a co-conspirator.

I looked up at the sky. The sun was moving westward. I estimated we had about four hours of daylight left.

"We'd best get started then," I said and stepped forward, to get Edwin and Nola moving.

Edwin still had the map and he hustled a little to get in front. I fell in behind him and Nola behind me. I was grateful it wasn't a forest. Not that there were a lot of heavily forested areas around here, but I just never liked to be anywhere that I could only see trees around me. Being among trees threw my mind right back to that day when the fairies or whatever they were changed my life.

We followed a fairly wide, well-developed trail for a while. Edwin stopped suddenly and peered at the map. He huffed out a breath and turned to take what I guessed might be an animal trail through the brush. Nola and I glanced at each other. We shared a *this had better be worth it* look and followed him.

Some sort of hawk soared overhead, riding the thermals and probably looking for something to eat. A moment later it swooped down and when next I caught sight of the raptor, a large lizard dangled from its beak.

A lone coyote watched us from atop a nearby rise. I think we must have amused him or her, silly humans who didn't seem to have the first idea about where they were going. The coyote wasn't wrong.

We followed animal trails through brush and tall grass, pushing through yellow Wild Mustard and red Indian Paintbrush, up and down a steep canyon. After an hour or so, I heard Nola panting behind me. My knees were starting to protest this unaccustomed terrain. Edwin strode on like he was strolling in the park.

An outcropping of trees appeared a hundred yards or so in front of us. A thrill of nerves shot through me. This was the place. I felt it as strongly as if a sign with a big red X were stuck to a tree.

Edwin turned to Nola and me, put his finger to his lips and motioned us to come stand with him. He pointed on the map to a small square with a triangle on top drawn on the map—a house. A grove that surrounded the house was indicated by the kind of little bumpy circles people often used to mean trees. He looked from the map to the grove in front of us.

"Michael's there," I said quietly, and didn't doubt it.

Edwin seemed equally sure. I suspected that a gift for healing and the ability to make harpoons appear in his hands weren't the only special abilities he possessed. He'd been too confident in all the paths he'd chosen to be relying only on a sketchy map to get us to our destination.

We set off again, moving more cautiously than we had been. Even so, we startled a group of small, brown house sparrows rooting in the chaparral for bugs. We all froze. I figured Edwin and Nola were thinking the same thing I was —if the sudden flight of sparrows alerted the witches to our approach, we were cooked.

But anything could have startled the birds—a fox, a coyote, hikers with nothing on their minds but enjoying a bit of nature. Unless Miranda had told the witches we were coming. That was a thought I didn't want to pursue. I had to believe she'd been truthful with us. If not, we were probably heading into a trap.

We set off again and crossed the distance to the outer trees in the grove. My heartbeat sped. When Edwin stepped past the first tree, I was right behind him, walking into a Eucalyptus trees fun house of thick trunks, piles of fallen leaves, and large chunks of bark that made my mouth go dry. I bounced my gaze back and forth between Edwin's back and the ground, to keep from tripping over fallen branches or twisting my ankle in a gopher hole.

We hadn't been among the trees more than fifteen minutes or so when I spotted a small, ramshackle cabin that couldn't have imprisoned a rabbit if it wasn't cursed. The shack was wood sided with a tin roof that seemed likely to fly off with the first stiff breeze. The wood-plank door was centered to the front and had a window on either side. The windows had red floral curtains that were drawn tight together.

Nola rushed up beside Edwin who was still in the lead and held her hand up in a *wait* sign.

"The perimeter is enchanted," she said keeping her voice low. "I'll have to dissolve it for us to get inside the cabin."

I stared at her. I heard her words and understood them, but my brain felt muzzy and the words didn't seem to make sense. Edwin nodded though, so maybe it made sense to him. He didn't seem concerned about whatever it was Nola was saying.

The cabin didn't look so rundown when I glanced at it again. There was a chimney I hadn't noticed before with a pleasant gray smoke wafting skyward. Someone inside was cooking something that smelled really good. I was suddenly ravenous. I took a few quick steps toward the cabin hoping whoever was in there would share their food.

"Edwin. Grab her," Nola said, her words soft but urgent. "Don't move and don't let her go."

"What about you?" he asked.

"Curse-breaker, remember? Enchantment immune or I'd be pretty crappy at my job."

I had no idea what they were talking about. What enchantment? Edwin wrapped a strong hand around my left upper arm. I tried to shake it off so I could go in the cabin. I was so very hungry. Whatever was cooking smelled delicious. I struggled but couldn't pull my arm free.

"Turn me loose," I hissed at him.

He wouldn't let go.

Nola was kneeling on the ground, digging into the backpack she'd brought. "I know I packed rue."

Edwin stood beside me, his grip tightening on my arm. This was all his fault. He'd insisted we leave early, no time to eat, and he'd brought us here. Now, with the promise of food so near, he held me back. I swung around to face him and kneed him hard in the balls. He grunted but didn't let go of my arm.

Nola let out a breath and pulled to her feet. She held a bag of some dried leaves in one hand and a bottle of water in the other. She poured the leaves into the water and swirled the bottle to mix them. Her mixture didn't smell nearly as good as what was coming from the cabin.

I leaned over and bit Edwin's hand that was wrapped around my arm. "Jesus!" he said, gritting his teeth and keeping his voice low.

Nola unscrewed the cap on the bottle and splashed water on me, soaking my face and shirt.

I blinked, shocked by the water. The cabin was once again

a shack. The chimney with its friendly smoke was gone. I couldn't smell anything being cooked.

"The enchantment got you," Nola said quietly to me. "It's meant to draw in anyone who wanders too close and gets too curious. My guess is that the witches would then wipe the trespasser's memory at the very least. You're okay now."

Edwin was cradling his bitten right hand in his left and grimacing.

Heat rose in my cheeks. I touched his shoulder. "I'm so sorry. I don't know why I did that."

"Forget it," he said. "Not your fault."

I rolled my shoulders, trying to shake off the last of the enchantment. "I didn't feel it coming. I always feel magic long before it gets to me."

"Let it go, Shay," Edwin said, brushing away my confusion and concerns. "We have work to do."

I couldn't though. "Why weren't you affected?"

"Demigod," he said in much the same tone Nola had used to say curse-breaker.

That made me the weak link. The one whose head could be clouded by the witches' magic. I wouldn't get caught again though. I'd be on high alert for magic coming at us from here on out.

Nola was busy pouring the rest of the leafy water in a circle around the three of us.

"I don't have enough supplies to break this wide an enchantment, but the circle will purify and protect us. When we move forward, it will move with us."

"Good trick," Edwin muttered and slowly started toward the cabin again.

"I don't think the witches are in the cabin," Nola said. "They would have felt their enchantment being breached. It's not like witches to stand by when that happens."

As if that was their cue, half a dozen witches suddenly flew at us, dive-bombing from the trees. Seeing bodies flying toward you is guaranteed to make your heart thump. It's worse when you know they're witches wishing you ill, but they look just like your neighbors or people you see every day on the street.

One witch in a long skirt and gauzy blouse, her long wheat-colored hair streaming behind her, screeched as she angled to take out Nola. I summoned wind to hold her away. The witch hovered in the air, fury reddening her face.

One with brown hair and wearing an Einstein on a bicycle t-shirt screeched as she fell toward me, a thick branch in her hand held ready to strike. I summoned a second blast of air to blow her back into the trees.

Two witches dove toward Edwin. I unleashed a whirlwind on them and watched them spin and tumble head over heels as the wind blew them away until they were lost to our view.

"Can you get into the cabin?" I said to Nola. "Quickly?"

She nodded.

"Okay. I'll keep the witches busy. You and Edwin get Michael."

"I'll stay with you," Edwin said. "Nola doesn't need my help."

"She might if Michael is bound by more than magic," I said. "Nola can break the curse, but can she break chains if the witches are hedging their bets? What if Michael is behind a locked door? I don't think Nola has the strength to break one down."

Edwin reluctantly nodded. "I'll check with Nola, but if only magic binds Michael Rawlings, I'll be right back out to help you."

"Thanks," I said.

The two sprinted toward the cabin. Too late I realized

she'd taken the protective circle with her. If the witches threw spells my way, I had nothing but my elements to protect me. And the sun was setting. The witches would be harder to see in the coming dusk. I needed a distraction.

I considered setting fire to some of the eucalyptus trees to drive off the witches, but a fire could too easily spread. Flammable gas from the trees' oils could ignite into fireballs. Fire wasn't the answer.

Wind and water though, I could use those.

The witches had disappeared into the trees. In the corner of my eye I caught a shimmer among the leaves of a eucalyptus. Someone readying a spell. I summoned up water to make clouds and poured rain from them. Water broke magic. I sent the rain wiping through the trees on a fierce wind blowing outward from where I stood. The shimmer in the trees faded as the witch was blown from her perch before she could finish her spell.

Edwin sprang from the cabin's door toward me, ducking and holding a hand over his head in a vain attempt to keep the pounding rain off him. "Nola says the curse is strong and complicated. She'll need time to break it. You need to come inside. She can't protect you out here."

I could keep up my defense for a while, but not forever. And I didn't want to be trying to walk back out of the reserve in the dark. Nola needed to break Michael's curse as quickly as possible and her worrying about me wasn't going to help. Having us all in one place inside one of her protective circles made sense. I nodded and made a shooing motion to him with my hand. He caught my meaning and ran back to the cabin. As soon as he was inside, I called upon all the magic I had in me and summoned up a series of tornados I set spinning all around the outside of the cabin. Between the tornados and the trees, I summoned dark clouds and let their rain pour down. The witch's spells couldn't get through water to harm us.

I timed the spinning tornados and raced to the door in the few seconds that a calm path opened up, pulled the door open and slammed it shut behind me as soon as I was inside. And got my first glimpse of Michael Rawlings, the man who'd caused so much trouble.

21

First off, Michael Rawlings was too young for Lady as far as I was concerned. I knew now that Lady wasn't the forty years old that her bio claimed, but Michael didn't know that. Why he thought a grown woman would be attracted to someone who was mid-twenties at most and looked about twelve was beyond me.

He was tall, thin, and rangy, with collar-length sandy brown hair and blue eyes that might show intelligence once the curse was off him. Now those eyes looked sleepy or stoned as Michael stared straight ahead at nothing. I didn't think he'd even registered we were here.

He was good looking, I'd give him that, with the kind of bone structure that would let him grow into stunningly handsome eventually and would keep him attractive well into middle-age and beyond.

He sat in an overstuffed wingchair upholstered in lime green. The room also sported a stained, beige couch and a couple of plastic end tables, the kind you might use on a patio. I didn't know what the witches—or anyone else—did here, but I'd have thought the furniture would be better. At the back of the room, a door led to something.

"Bathroom," Nola said, seeing where my gaze had traveled. "Chemical toilet. No running water so we'll have to be careful with water needed for spells."

Nola sat on the couch, her backpack on her knees, rummaging through its contents. A thirty-two-ounce Coke bottle, refilled with what I guessed was water, sat on one of the plastic end tables.

Edwin had a smaller bottle in his hand. Bits of green leaves floated in the water—rue, maybe. He was walking the perimeter of the living room, sprinkling protection. Once he'd made a complete circuit, I felt my shoulders relax and the tension in my stomach ease. I trusted the tornados I'd summoned to stop the witches outside from invading the cabin, but it was wearing on me to keep up the magic.

Nola had pulled four little bags from her pack. Two were clear plastic baggies and I could see more rue, and some yellow flower bits—yarrow perhaps. Two of the bags were suede and drawn closed with purple twine. She was singing to herself under her breath as she mixed a pinch of this and a dab of that into little plastic spray bottles also drawn from her pack. I could only make out a few of the words.

"Rue and bay leaf,
mumble mumble and twine,
mumble-y mumble bits
mumble the divine."

She pulled a bottle of some kind of essential oil from her bag and added a few drops to a couple of the leaf and water mixtures. The smell of cinnamon wafted in the air.

Evidently finished with her preparations, Nola got up, picked up the spray bottles, and walked over to stand in front of Michael, who still sat slumped and dazed-looking in the ugly lime-green chair.

Edwin stood a little behind her, watching over her shoulder. I could see what she was doing from where I sat on the couch and stayed there.

Nola turned and handed all the bottles but one to Edwin. He looked surprised but held them. They looked tiny in his big hands. Nola started singing softly again as she spritzed Michael with whatever was in the first bottle. Done, she handed that bottle to Edwin, and took another from him. She spritzed Michael again, but without singing this time.

When she'd finished spraying him with water from the fourth and final bottle, he blinked rapidly a few times and straightened up in the chair. His eyes widened. I saw the fear in them.

"Who are you?" he said. "Where are the witches?"

Edwin stepped forward and held out his hand. "Hey dude. Feeling better? I'm Edwin." He indicated me and Nola with short bobs of his chin. "That's Shay, and that's Nola. We're here to take you home."

Michael blinked rapidly, trying to take in Edwin's words, I thought, as he struggled to his feet. He was wobbly and had to put one hand on the arm of the chair to stay upright.

"Are the witches still here?" Michael asked, his voice shaky. "They won't let you go. They for sure won't let me go. They want something I don't have and won't tell them where it is."

"Miranda told us," I said. "She's how we knew where you were. Edwin's right, we're here to take you home. Do what we ask, and no harm will come to you."

He blinked again, taking that in. "Miranda sent you?"

I nodded and held out my hand. It was pretty clear Michael knew what had happened to him and why. It was also pretty clear he wasn't sure if he should trust us or not. He took my hand, but doubt clouded his eyes.

"I thought I knew all of my sister's friends."

I cleared my throat, wondering if honesty was really the wisest move. "Edwin and I work for Lady Califia. She hired me to retrieve the Mermaid's Lament."

Michael stiffened. He pulled his hand free of mine. "I don't have it."

"I know that," I said. "Miranda says she knows where it is. We bring you to her, she gives us the necklace, everyone's happy."

He narrowed his eyes. "Even Lady."

"Especially Lady."

"And Calypso?" he said.

"She says she's fine with it. And both have promised that no harm will come to you if Calypso gets the necklace back by Saturday at dawn."

"What day is today?" he asked.

"Friday," I said.

He ran his hand over his hair, taking that in.

"Let's go see your sister," I said.

He tensed. "The witches?"

Yeah. The damn witches. I'd let the tornadoes die down once the cabin's interior was protected. I knew I didn't have the energy left to keep wind spinning around us all the way back to the car. I turned to Nola. "Can you do a protection circle around us?

She pressed her lips together, thinking. "Probably not. I mean, I could certainly do a mobile protection circle, but chances are the witches will follow. If one of us so much as stumbled and broke the circle, the whole thing would dissolve."

And the witches would be on us in a hot second.

I could blow them away with wind but unless I sent them miles and miles away, which was probably beyond my abilities though I'd never actually tried, they'd be back before we reached the car.

Water seemed the best bet. Rain that just needed to fall on the four of us was easier to control than wind, and water disrupted magic. Not my magic, since I was the conduit, but it would interrupt and destroy any spell or curse the witches sent our way. Which still left us vulnerable to physical attack. I glanced at Edwin. If the witches, who outnumbered us, went for a physical attack, most of our defense would have to come from him.

"I hope no one minds getting wet," I said. "We'll be heavily rained on the moment we step out the door."

"What?" Michael said. "I don't hear rain."

The other two simply nodded. Edwin reached for the knob and pulled the door open.

22

The witches were waiting outside. I counted six crouched in the limbs of the Eucalyptus trees. One cackled and set herself in a position that I was pretty sure meant she was going to launch herself toward us. I summoned up a hell of a rain to pour down on the four of us. The witch swore and repositioned herself in the tree.

Yeah. I could see it already. Things were going to get physical.

"Edwin," I said. "That trick you did with the harpoons. Could you do it now? Make three? One for each of us."

Three, because I didn't trust that Michael would know what to do with a weapon. Nor did I completely trust him not to turn on us and try to break away.

Again, I had no idea how he did it, but a spear—not a harpoon this time—appeared in Edwin's hand. He gave it to Nola. A second spear appeared, and he handed it to me. The spear was longer than I was, maybe six feet, about an inch around, and heavier than I'd expected. I jiggled it around a bit to find a comfortable balance point. When I looked up again, Edwin had a wicked looking sword in his hands. Hands, because I'm sure that even for him, it took two to hold and wield the thing.

I glanced up in the trees. The witches seemed surprised at the suddenly appearing weapons. Good, I thought. Maybe they'll leave us alone.

The rain was coming hard enough that the dirt was turning to mud where we stood.

"Let's go," I said.

Edwin took point. Nola and I kept Michael between us. We didn't frog march him or even crowd him, but we made sure we were close. I was right-handed, but Nola, I noticed now, was left-handed. We were positioned so each of us held our spear in our dominant hand, spears to the outside with Michael in between.

A blur of motion caught my eye. The witches were gliding from tree to tree as we walked, staying even or ahead of us. Waiting for the perfect moment to attack, I thought.

We were almost out of the copse of Eucalyptus trees. Once we made it back to open land, the witches would lose their vantage spots in the branches.

The witches screamed. All of them. All at once. The sound was primal, animal-like. The hairs on the back of my neck stood up and adrenaline rushed through me. Before I could get two hands on my spear, three witches had dropped from the trees. One landed on Nola's back, knocking her to the ground. Edwin spun and hacked off her head with one blow of his sword. Blood spurted from the wound. Nola sat up and crabwalked away from the dead witch, but not fast enough to avoid the witch's blood on her skin and clothes. The rain was beating down hard enough to help wash the blood off Nola.

The witch who'd aimed for me missed as I spun and pushed Michael up toward Edwin. The witch crashed into the muddy ground but was up and on her feet again in a heartbeat like some damn MMA fighter. She bared her teeth and sprung toward me, rabbit-like.

I didn't think. Didn't consider the consequences. I shoved the spear into her belly and pushed until I hit spine at the back. When I turned to check on my companions, the third witch lay dead at Edwin's feet.

Branches in the trees around us shook as the remaining witches scattered away from us. I grabbed Michael by the arm and ran until I was free of the trees and out in open land again.

He stared at me wide-eyed.

"You killed them," Michael said.

"Not by choice," I said. "We wouldn't have harmed them if they hadn't attacked."

Or if you hadn't been stupid and stolen the necklace in the first place, I thought.

He swallowed hard and nodded.

Edwin and Nola came out of the trees and stood with us.

"They won't attack again in the open," Edwin said. "At least I don't think they will."

"Probably not," I said. "I'll keep the rain going so they can't get us with magic."

In the few minutes Edwin and Nola had been out of my sight, Edwin had acquired a leather back strap sheath for the sword, which now rode high on his back. Nola still carried her spear. Mine was in the witch I'd killed. Edwin hadn't conjured up another for me. I hoped that meant I wasn't going to need another one.

We walked back to the car as fast as we could, still keeping an eye out for the witches. We were all drenched and half drowned from the rain by the time we reached the road.

The sun had nearly gone, and the temperature had dropped. Michael shivered so hard his teeth chattered.

I stopped the rain and summoned up a warm breeze, to help dry and warm us. Edwin went around to the back of the SUV, pulled open the hatch door, and pulled out towels for us all. I gave him a look.

He shrugged. "You work for Lady, it's a good idea to have supplies for many occasions."

We dried off as best we could. Nola hadn't spoken since the first witch had died. I was pretty sure she'd never seen someone killed in front of her like that. It was an ugly, ugly sight, one I'd been lucky to only see twice before this. I didn't want a fourth time.

Nola claimed the shotgun seat. I was about to pull open the back door when the crunch of feet on gravel made me spin around and look down the road.

Saylor.

And his four henchmen, the same ones I'd seen at Scotty's the other day.

Michael stood a few paces behind me. Two of Saylor's minions ran with incredible speed and grabbed him, one on each side, and were dragging him away almost before I registered what was happening. I started to sprint toward Michael, but another of Saylor's henchmen, a big, shaven-head brute of a man slammed into me, driving me to the ground. He fell on top of me and pinned my arms at my sides.

I had to make the two that had Michael let him loose. I summoned my will and my control over earth and made the ground shake under them. From the side of my eye, I saw Edwin bolt from the car and punch Saylor in the gut. Nola let out a small yell, but I couldn't see her to know what was happening. I brought my knee up hard and caught the brute lying on top of me between the legs. He swore loudly and rolled off me to clutch at his crotch.

I scrambled up to my feet and rumbled the land beneath the running minions and Michael, making it buck and heave. One minion stumbled, but he kept hold of Michael's arm and used Michael's body to steady himself.

But it slowed all three long enough for me to send a blast of wind to blow dirt in their eyes and to send the earth beneath their feet heaving up and down again. I ran toward the three. Michael was smart enough to use the moment his captors were off balance and blinded to yank his arms free of both men and give them each a shove. They fell to the ground while Michael stayed on his feet. I ran toward them.

Michael hesitated half a nanosecond and sprinted across the road toward a residential area. I chased after him, lengthening my strides to catch him before he could reach the homes and hide himself in some shrubbery or take turn after turn onto too many streets for me to follow, but he was faster than I would ever be. By the time I reached the first street, he'd vanished from view.

I stood in front of someone's multi-million-dollar home, my chest heaving from the exertion, thinking *fuck!*

23

I wasn't helping anyone standing there getting angry at myself. I trotted back toward the car, to see if I could help Edwin or Nola.

Edwin's nose was bleeding, and Nola was fuming when I reached them. Saylor and his minions had vanished.

"Where'd they go?" I said.

Edwin held up an arm and pointed down the road.

"They had a driver waiting," Nola said. "He drove up. Saylor and his goons jumped in and they sped away."

Fuck, again.

"Are you okay?" I asked Edwin and was surprised at the depth of my concern.

"Fine," he said, his word clipped and his voice cold.

"I have a cloth in my pack," Nola said. She looked around to find where her pack had been flung by the henchman, retrieved it, and rummaged inside.

I'd already grabbed one of the towels we'd used to dry off and handed it to Edwin.

He dabbed at the blood on his face and still running from

his nose. Nola gently pulled it from her hand and replaced it with a cloth from her bag.

I guessed it was good to be a demigod. The blood stopped flowing within seconds. Or maybe there was something magical about the cloth. Or maybe he used his healer abilities on himself. I'd ask about that later. We needed to decide what to do now that Michael was gone.

In my mind, there was only one thing to do. We had to go to Miranda, tell her what had happened, and convince her to remove the curse from the necklace and hand it over.

"We can take you home first," I said to Nola. "This could turn into a very long night."

She propped her right hand on her hip. "Not a chance. This is the most fun I've had in a while. Well, except for the killing witches part. I could have done without that." She smiled the tiniest bit. "And, you know, I am a curse-breaker. You might find it useful to have me along in case this Miranda person gets bulky about uncursing the pearls."

Why I hadn't thought of that was beyond me. I guessed I had it in my mind that Miranda had to break the curse she'd laid on the Mermaid's Lament. But twice now I'd seen Nola break curses others had set. It seemed logical she could break Miranda's curse as well. We were a team now, for this job, each of us bringing something the others lacked. It was only right that we should be together to recover the prize.

But Miranda still had to hand over the necklace. Getting that to happen was going to be a challenge since we didn't have Michael to trade for it and time was running out.

From the back seat as we were traveling down the hill toward the beach Nola piped up with, "What are you going to tell Miranda, Shay? She's expecting you to bring her brother to her, right?"

Edwin turned his head slightly to look at me. "I was wondering the same thing."

I opened my mouth to answer but shut it again. My mind spun a bunch of possible methods, but none of them seemed right. Finally, I said, "I'm not quite sure yet, but I'll think of something."

"I hope so," Edwin said. "The Mermaid's Lament has to be in Calypso's hands by dawn or—"

"I know the stakes," I said testily. And then, "Sorry. I didn't mean to snap at you."

Edwin shrugged. "Snap away. Just come up with a solution."

It was nearing eight pm by the time we pulled up in front of Miranda's cute little Victorian. Lights were on inside, which probably meant she was home. Alone, or with company we'd have to get rid of? Or maybe Michael was there. If he'd gone to her house after eluding me, that would make things easier.

"Do you want to go up by yourself?" Nola asked me as we pulled into a parking spot by the curb. "She might feel overwhelmed if we three descend on her."

"No," I said. "We're in this together. Besides, I think it would be good for her to feel overwhelmed. Intimidated might be even better. Edwin, you can do intimidating, right?"

He smiled and then set his face into a hard, frozen glare that sent a ripple of nerves up my breastbone.

I blew out a breath. "Yeah. You can definitely do intimidating."

His face relaxed again.

We got out of the car and walked up the driveway and then the little flat-stone path to her front door.

"Knock politely or pound?" Edwin said.

"Definitely a polite knock." I reached up and rapped my knuckles against the door.

Miranda threw the door open and looked expectantly at us.

"Where's Michael? You couldn't free him?" Her voice chilled. "You came here to tell me the witches still have my brother!"

"May we come in?" I said, my voice friendly and light.

Miranda froze a moment, seeming to need time to decide. I knew I wasn't one of her favorite people. I wasn't sure what I would do if she started to close the door in our faces. Blow it open and storm in, I supposed. Not a good way to start with her.

Miranda sighed and opened the door all the way. She stood aside to let us in.

"We found Michael," I said. Best to start off with the good news, I thought. "We freed him from the witches and the curse. Nola," I glanced her way, "broke the curse."

Miranda's shoulders and back visibly relaxed. "Where is he now? Why didn't he come with you? He wasn't hurt, was he?"

"No, he was fine the last I saw him," I said.

"Good," she said, and then, "Why isn't he here?"

I made that flip of the hand motion that meant I didn't have an answer she was going to like. "We were attacked when we got back to the car. Michael got free of his captors but ran off. I hoped he'd come here."

"He didn't." A sly look crossed her face. "But you're hoping I'll give you the Mermaid's Lament anyway." She laughed under her breath. "That isn't going to happen. You bring Michael here and I'll fetch the necklace and break the curse I've put on it. You're not getting it any other way." She crossed her arms over her chest as if to emphasize her refusal.

Edwin had put on his intimidation face at the door and kept it on. I didn't think Miranda had half-noticed he was even there.

"Miranda Rawlings," he said in a voice I'd never heard from him before. A voice that was low, rumbling, and carried so much threat in it that the hair on the back of my neck stood up. He might not have the power of persuasion like Lady did, but he could do scary really well.

Miranda clearly heard the threat as well. She drew herself up tall.

"Who are you that I should be frightened?" she said. "My magic is strong. Those who oppose or threaten me live to regret it."

Edwin chuckled, a sound so cold it made me rethink everything I thought I knew about him.

"I doubt Lady Califia and the goddess Calypso are among those your paltry magic can touch," he said. "But fine, hold on to that string of pearls. A word in certain ears and the witches of your coven will know you have the Mermaid's Lament. Both goddesses will know, as well as Calypso's son, Saylor, who also very much wants those pearls." He turned to me. "And who else did you say was after the necklace?"

"There was that ghoul."

"Right." Edwin said. "Ghouls are such nasty sorts, eaters of the dead and all." He smiled coldly at Miranda. "I'm sure the ghoul would find you a tasty snack."

I set my hand lightly on Miranda's arm. "Give us the necklace and we will all go to bed safe and happy tonight."

She kept the defiant pose on her face, but I could see Edwin had frightened her and she was cracking.

I saw something else, too. "You never planned to give me the necklace, did you? You thought you could get Michael back and keep the Mermaid's Lament. How did you plan to do that?"

Edwin's voice kept its harsh edge. "Tell the truth, Miranda."

Nola said, "I'm not too shabby at casting spells. A truth spell might be just what's needed here."

Miranda gaped at Nola who was shifting her backpack around so she could get into it for supplies.

"No," Miranda said forcefully. "No spell."

Edwin smiled and held out a hand toward her. His voice softened as he repeated what he'd said before. "Tell the truth, Miranda."

She drew in a shaky breath and let it out slowly. "I had a copy made. I was going to give you the paste copy and take the real necklace for myself. And for Michael. I thought we'd have plenty of time to disappear before the fraud was discovered."

I wondered what Miranda was so afraid of revealing if she were under a truth spell that she'd tell us the truth about the necklace to avoid the spell? I didn't doubt she'd told the truth. It felt too true. When I glanced at Edwin, I could see he believed her too.

Did she fear saying something about the Mermaid's Lament? About Michael? About a thing we knew nothing about, and she was afraid we'd discover? And what had the brother and sister planned if they'd managed to keep the real pearls? Selling it to the highest bidder?

"Why don't you go get the necklace for us?" Edwin said his voice pitched so his request seemed the most intelligent and reasonable thing in the world. "We'll keep it safe."

Her shoulders slumped suddenly, as if she were a marionette whose strings had been cut.

"I'll get it."

She disappeared into another room.

"She's not going out a window or back door, is she?" Nola asked.

Edwin shook his head. "Nope. She's gone to get the necklace."

"The real one, or the fake?"

"Shay will know which the moment Miranda hands them over," he said. "She can sense things when she's in contact with solid objects."

Nola shot me a look, and I shrugged. I didn't think I'd told Edwin that, but Lady knew. I'd told her that first day in her office. She must have told Edwin.

Had the Mermaid's Lament been here all along? No, I thought. Miranda had gone somewhere and fetched them while we'd been out freeing Michael. If the necklace had been here when I'd come before, her demeanor would have been different.

Miranda returned with a thin white box in her hands. She opened it and held the Mermaid's Lament out.

"Have you removed your curse?" Edwin asked.

"Yeah," she said.

Something in her tone set my senses on edge. I took the necklace from her and cradled the pearls in my hands. Their magic hummed against my skin. I nodded.

"Thank you," he said softly. "We'll be going now. I hope Michael gets in touch with you soon. If I hear anything about where he is, I'll tell you and do my best to get him back to you."

Miranda's eyes brimmed with tears, but I didn't know if they were in gratitude for Edwin's promise or in pain that she'd given up the pearls.

24

A sliver of moon rode among the stars by the time we turned onto the private road to Lady's house. Lights were on in the house, but instead of seeming welcoming, there was something cold about the gleam. A nervous twitter flew up my breastbone. I clutched my purse with the Mermaid's Lament inside close to my chest.

"This doesn't feel right," I said.

"No," Edwin said as he slowed the car as we entered the long driveway, "it doesn't."

"It's too quiet," Nola said.

Edwin nodded. "I'd have expected Lady to come out to meet us when she heard my car. She'd want to know if we'd gotten the necklace or not."

"Do we stay, or do we go?" Nola asked.

"Stay," Edwin and I said in unison.

"And fight," I added, because it seemed clear to me that something was amiss and that something was probably Saylor. Or maybe Calypso—the sea goddess wanting to ensure that Lady couldn't return the Mermaid's Lament by grabbing it from us before we could hand it off. Or someone, or something, else. It seemed an awful lot of entities were after the necklace.

Edwin turned the engine off but sat a moment, not moving to open the driver-side door.

"I'm going to count to three," he said. "On three, we all jump from the car at the same time and race for the house."

I heard Nola shift in the back seat and assumed she was doing the same thing I was—taking hold of the door handle in preparation.

"One," Edwin said. "Two. Three."

We swung our doors open and leaped from the car. Nola and I ran for the front door. Edwin, I saw, had veered left, as if to go around the side of the house to the back yard.

He'd planned that all along, I thought. Why?

There wasn't much time to wonder. A scream from overhead made me look up.

"Ghouls," Nola yelled.

A half dozen of them. The single ghoul who'd run my car off the road had led me to believe she was employed by someone even a ghoul found disreputable. That ghoul had sent me back to Miranda. Miranda sent us to the witches. Were they all in it together—Michael, Miranda, the ghouls, and the witches? Working together—to what end?

Ghouls are part of the djinn family and the fuckers can fly. They flew at Nola and me, soaring down from the treetops, their rotted-corpse faces twisted in maniacal glee. Fire wouldn't hurt them; they were fire themselves from somewhere in the dim recesses of time. But water could harm, maybe kill them. Could ghouls be killed?

My purse strap was over my shoulder, the purse flapping against my side. I shifted it to my chest and flung my arms over it to secure it in place and ran a zigzag route toward the house. I zigged and a ghoul who'd focused his flight line to collide square on with me only hit my right shoulder on his way to crash onto the driveway.

A different ghoul dove at Nola. She ducked in time to avoid being rammed into and the ghoul flew past her. She popped right back up to her full, tiny height and pointed toward the sky.

"Witches incoming," she yelled.

I was busy focusing my power to soak the ghouls and didn't spare even a second to look up. There was a pond the size of an Olympic swimming pool in Lady's garden. Faster and easier to use the pool water than to condense moisture from the air, make clouds, and then rain.

"Get the fuck off me," I heard Nola say.

I glanced over and saw two ghouls had pinned her to the ground. I didn't know if Nola had any magic beyond curse breaking and some light spell casting. One of the ghouls had his scarred, fleshy hand over Nola's mouth and nose, trying to suffocate her. Another sat on her chest.

Okay, water for the ghouls, fire for the witches.

Except the witches flew right past us, around the side and toward the back of the house, the way Edwin had gone.

I concentrated on forming the water from Lady's pond into a large ball. I used swirling air around the ball to help hold the shape and called the water to me.

A ghoul landed on my back, knocking the air from my lungs, and dragged me to the ground. I flipped over and shoved the ghoul hard in the chest to knock him off and scrambled to my feet. The ghoul was on his feet almost as quickly. He drew back his arm, bony fingers closed in a fist, ready to slug me. I ducked under his punch and, hugging my purse to my side, ran toward Nola. I needed us together to draw all the ghouls to one place.

I'd lost control of the water when the ghoul had dropped

me. I heard the water splatter on the ground and felt it begin to sink into the dirt. I focused my magic and called the water back out of the soil and into the air.

Magic surged in me, roiling through my body, desperate to manifest itself somehow. Strong emotions did that to me. I called the water from the pipes running from the street to the house.

Pipes began bursting in the yard from the pressure of the water rushing from the street toward Lady's house. If the pipes at my own house hadn't burst, I never would have thought to do this. I didn't want the pipes breaking inside her house, though. I pulled the water already in the house and the water from the street to meet in the front yard. A geyser shot up, rising maybe fifteen feet and then splashing down, drenching Nola, the ghouls, and me.

The ghouls screamed in pain. They scattered to get away from the geyser.

But they were slow, the water weakening them. They ran not like swift-footed ghouls but lurched like TV zombies. A few tried to take to the air but landed face down on the wet grass with more water pouring over them. Steam began rising from their bodies.

I pulled the water that remained in the pond, added it to the water that had been in the first water ball, and pulled it all to me as a surging flood.

More pipes burst, sending more water spurting into the air. I grabbed that water and added it to the surge. Lady's front yard, where we were, was wide but the ghouls were so slow now they hadn't gotten far apart when the wave hit.

The surge hit me, too, knocking me off my feet and dragging me across the grass-covered lawn. My purse was torn from my shoulder and dragged away by the wild water. I struggled to get my head up and breathe, but the current was too fast. I didn't know where Nola was but assumed the water had knocked her over as well. I had no idea where Edwin was. He'd disappeared around the side of the house and hadn't returned since the witches had chased after him. I hoped he was okay.

The water pushed me toward the street. Luckily, it was a private road, not one with traffic. My lungs were starting to burn from holding my breath. My shoulder slammed into a tree trunk. I flung my arms around the trunk and managed to pull myself up enough to grab a gulp of air before the surging water tore me away and into the gravel-lined road.

I saw my purse, with the Mermaid's Lament inside, rise to the surface. I grabbed for it, but it was out of my reach. Moments later it disappeared under the water. I tracked the line I thought it had taken and scrambled after it as best I could. At least the water was pushing me and my purse in the same direction. I always bought purses that zippered and kept the zipper closed. Thank God for that, I thought. At least the necklace wouldn't fall out and be carried who knew where by the water.

Thank goodness for my jeans and shoes, which were saving my legs and feet from getting torn up on the gravel the water was pushing me over. My hands weren't faring as well. They were going to hurt like hell when this was over. I jammed my palms down behind me, bent my knees and put my feet flat on the road, and pushed.

I got my head, shoulders and chest above the water just in time to grab a breath of air and to see a dragon fly overhead.

A damn dragon. Witches and ghouls weren't bad enough?

The dragon seemed to have a target in mind, but I couldn't see what it was aiming for. My purse? Was this one more entry into the Mermaid's Lament sweepstakes? A wild-card player coming late onto the field because witches, ghouls, and the son of a goddess weren't enough?

Fuck. Fuck. Fuck.

I pulled my focus together and stilled the water in the pipes and began sending the pond water back where it had come from. I thought I should send wind to knock the dragon off whatever trajectory it was on, but it was taking everything I had to control the water.

Where had the witches gone? Had they cast some spell and coalesced into the dragon now diving for something on the lawn? This new world I'd stumbled into was insane.

25

The dragon dove straight toward Nola.
Before I could work up enough wind to knock the dragon away, it swept down and grabbed Nola by the back of her shirt and lifted her into the air. She hung from the dragon's mouth like a child's stuffed toy. I couldn't tell if she was unconscious or dead.

I swallowed hard. If it was either, it was my fault for bringing her into the case. I didn't know her family to notify them. I didn't even know her last name.

Jesus.

I scrambled to my feet, slipping once on the wet ground before I found my footing. The dragon, carrying Nola, had flown over the roof of Lady's house and dropped down somewhere behind it. I wanted to run to the back, see if she was alive. If she was behind the house. The damn dragon could have flown off anywhere with her.

I spotted my purse lying caught between a tall tree and a high hedge. I couldn't leave it. The pearls were inside. Okay. Grab my purse, then look for Nola. And Edwin. Where the hell was Edwin?

Saylor stepped out from the backside of the hedge. Fucking Saylor. Where had he come from? He must have been here a while. His hair and clothes were wet.

I lunged for my purse, snatched it up, and took several steps back. I was soaked. My hands burned from where the gravel had torn the skin. Nola had to be found. Maybe a dragon dealt with. I was in no mood for Saylor.

"Back off," I said as I readied fire, in case he didn't quite catch what the tone in my voice meant.

His eyes were as hard as twin coals, but his mouth curved in a smile. "You have it, don't you? The Mermaid's Lament is in your handbag. I'm going to walk over to you now and you will hand the necklace to me."

I felt the pull of his words, the desire to do what he said. Evidently he'd inherited some of those godly persuasion powers. But his were nothing compared to the persuasion powers Lady had, and I'd overcome those the day she interviewed me.

"I think not," I said with a scoff.

Saylor kept smiling as he walked toward me. "But you will. You want to give the necklace to me. You want to give it to me as much as you've ever wanted to do anything. Handing me the pearls will make you very happy. It's what you want to do."

Almost involuntarily my eyes strayed to my purse. I almost undid the zipper. Almost, but I didn't.

But Saylor had seen where my gaze had gone.

"You want me to have them. Just stand there, doing nothing, and I'll take care of everything."

I had to do something. Throw down a wall of fire between Saylor and me. Make the earth shake. Something. But I so wanted to simply stand there and watch, making no effort.

And I might have, but I flung a fireball the size of my two fists together straight toward his head instead.

Saylor laughed as he ducked. I was not in the mood for his laughter.

I conjured up two more fireballs, one for each hand, and threw one high and one low.

Saylor danced away from them and before I could ready another blast, the dragon reappeared and swooped down. It grabbed my purse with its mouth, pulling it from my hands, and soared away. Once again, the dragon flew over Lady's house and seemed to drop down somewhere behind it. The back of the yard bordered on a land preserve. The dragon could be anywhere.

"Nice going, asshat," I growled. "Now neither of us has the Mermaid's Lament. Your mother's not going to be happy, and neither is Lady."

Saylor laughed again, but there wasn't much humor in it. "I think Lady will be pleased."

"Oh? Why do you think that?"

Saylor's gaze shifted away from me and focused on the side of the house. I didn't know if it was a trick to get me looking in another direction so he could attack or if there was really something worth seeing. Nola maybe? More likely Edwin who hadn't been seen since he disappeared along the side of the house with witches chasing after him. I hoped it would be Edwin and he'd be all right. I glanced quickly over my shoulder.

Edwin held up my still dripping purse. Nola stood beside him.

Saylor made a scoffing sound and I looked back at him.

"You didn't know, did you?" he said.

"Know what?"

"Edwin has a dragon form. All the demigods can change.

It's in our DNA. The gods and goddesses can be practically anything they want. Edwin only has the dragon."

"Check that the necklace is still inside," I called to Edwin as I came to grips with this new information. A dragonshifter. Fuck me. And he'd pulled Nola from the water and saved her.

Edwin unzipped my bag and rummaged around inside. Men have no idea all the bits and bobs women carry in their purses. He finally pulled out the soggy box that all but fell apart in his hands and held up the Mermaid's Lament.

Saylor made this weird rumbling noise deep in his throat. The hairs on the back of my neck stood up. Did he have another form as well? Was I about to see him change?

Instead he burst forward, covering the distance between he and Edwin so fast that Edwin didn't even get the smile off his face before Saylor tackled him to the ground. Saylor grabbed the necklace and leaped up. Nola reached for him, but he shoved her away and ran back in my direction.

A car was coming up the drive. I didn't dare turn to look and see who it was. Lady maybe? The getaway driver for Saylor?

I focused my mind and made the earth under his feet buck and tremble. Saylor stumbled but kept to his feet and continued running. I upped the ante. The ground rose up and sank back down, then shimmied side to side. The front yard was in turmoil. Flowers were uprooted and tossed aside. Chunks of grass flew into the air. I had trouble keeping my own balance.

But Saylor fell.

A car door slammed behind me at the same moment a horrid shriek sounded from somewhere above the trees.

A lone witch, who must have been waiting all this time, dove from the branches and landed on Saylor's back. She grabbed the necklace and tugged, but Saylor wouldn't let go.

They rolled and tumbled in the soggy grass, both of them getting wet, both yanking on the necklace.

"Stop," Lady yelled. "Damn it, stop. Being cursed might have weakened—"

The witch gritted her teeth and pulled. The string broke. Pearls scattered across the lawn.

The witch jumped to her feet and gave Saylor a hard kick in the ribs.

"Idiot," she snarled.

She turned a harsh eye on Edwin. "Where are my sisters?"

"The hell with your sisters," Lady said.

Edwin grinned. "In the back. Bespelled. Care to join them?"

And who had cast that? Edwin or Nola?

The witch screeched and turned. She ran toward a tree and *up* the trunk. In seconds she had disappeared among the branches and leaves. Seconds later she reappeared at the top branch, leaped into the air, and seemed to just disappear.

I've seen lots of magic, but that was a first.

26

Lady stared at the ruined remains of her yard and sighed. Nola and I were wet and bedraggled. Saylor, who'd slowly pulled himself to his feet, was wet and worn out from fighting with the witch on the lawn. The pearls lay scattered in the grass. His gaze bounced from pearl to pearl. Lady shifted her gaze to him.

"What are you doing here, Saylor?"

He didn't look up, but his voice came out strong. "I came for my mother's pearls, of course."

Damn. That boy could lie like nobody's business.

"Well, you didn't manage that very well, did you?" Lady said, crossing her arms over her chest.

Saylor raised his head to look at Lady. The heat in his eyes could have burned through steel. "My mother sent me to retrieve the pearls."

"That doesn't make sense," I said. "Lady will return them to her at first light. Calypso didn't need to send you to steal them."

Saylor laughed. It was a harsh, ragged sound.

"I see," Lady said. "Calypso meant for it to be impossible for me to return them."

I shook my head. "I don't think so. I think Calypso doesn't know Saylor is here."

Edwin and Nola began picking up loose pearls in the wet grass.

"Oh, leave it. Leave it," Lady said, the flick of her hand showing her anger and impatience. "We'll gather them later. Not that it matters. The pearls can never be restrung in the right order. The spell is lost."

Edwin stood next to me. I leaned over and asked in a soft voice, "Why can't they be restrung? Someone devised the spell originally. Why can't it be cast again?"

"That sorcerer is dead," he said quietly. "Drowned."

Drowned—by Calypso? So the sorcerer couldn't enchant another set of pearls or anything else? So only she would have the magic he'd made?

Lady drew in a deep breath. Evidently, she'd made up her mind about what to do next.

"I think it's time for a drive," she said to Edwin. She turned and locked her gaze on Saylor. Her voice grew chill and hard. "Shall we go talk to your mother, ask her if she sent you here tonight or not?"

The fear emanating from Saylor was so strong I could practically taste it. He was in trouble and knew it. Big time trouble. I didn't pity him one little bit.

Nola sidled up next to me. "Weird to say, but I've had enough excitement for one day. I'd like to go home now. Would that be all right?"

"I don't see why not," I said. Lady didn't need Nola to find Calypso and tell her what Saylor had done. She didn't need me either.

"Um," I said to get Lady's attention. "Nola would like to

go home, if you don't need her." I paused. "I'd like to go home as well."

Lady pursed her lips. Her gaze never left Saylor. "Nola may go. You, Shayna, will accompany Edwin, Saylor, and me."

Nola and I gave each other little shrugs. She pulled her miraculously dry phone from her pack and ordered an Uber, which was pretty much what I wished I were doing at the moment. I also thought that if Nola kept her phone safe and dry through some sort of spell, I'd like to have her bespell my purse so it couldn't be stolen, or opened by anyone but me, and that everything inside would be safe no matter what happened. That would be useful.

Lady closed her hand around Saylor's arm and gave him a shove. "Get in the car."

Saylor obeyed like a boy being sent to his room, knowing he'd committed a family crime.

"Will you be all right here alone until your driver comes?" I asked Nola.

She nodded.

I got in the car on the shotgun side. Lady sat with Saylor in the back. Edwin didn't ask *where to?* He simply backed the car out of the driveway and turned to go down the gravel road.

I wasn't surprised when we arrived at the same stretch of beach where we'd last spoken with Calypso. Lady sent Saylor as clear a '*Don't even think of trying something*' glare as I've ever seen and got out of the back seat. She walked around the car and opened Saylor's door. Saylor climbed out and stood by the car. Edwin had gotten out as well. Lady nodded to him and he took hold of one of Saylor's arms.

It was deep night now and as dark as pitch on the road. I

wasn't looking forward to stumbling my way down the twisty path to the water. I was thinking about summoning up a fireball to provide some light when light burst around us as if someone had turned a switch. The light didn't extend more than five or ten feet around us, but it was plenty bright to let us see our way. Lady's doing, I thought. The four of us walked down to the shore.

As before, Lady called a fish and told it we needed to speak with Calypso, and it was urgent. The last time Lady had sent a fish to ask Calypso to appear, she'd come immediately. Now we stood by the shore, the waves lapping on the sand, and waited.

And waited.

Lady crossed her arms over her chest and tapped her foot impatiently.

Finally, Calypso arrived, riding a dolphin. She surely did like to make an entrance.

The sea goddess dismounted into the water and glided to the shore.

"It's not yet dawn," she said. "Are you returning my necklace early?"

"I have sad news," Lady said. "The Mermaid's Lament has been destroyed. The string was broken during a tug-of-war between Saylor and a witch, both of whom were after your necklace. The pearls themselves are scattered on my front lawn."

The sea goddess regarded the goddess of California for a long moment.

"I see," she said and shifted her gaze to her son. "Is this true?"

Saylor puffed out his chest. "I was trying to get it back for you."

Calypso put on hand on her hip. "Were you?"

"In truth," Lady said, "it seems your child wanted the Mermaid's Lament for purposes of his own."

Calypso's gaze remained locked on Saylor. "Oh?"

"Evidently he was jealous of our near immortality and wanted the same for himself," Lady continued. "It is only through the great efforts of Shayna, Edwin, and one other that the necklace was recovered at all. They brought it to my house so I could deliver it to you. Unfortunately, Saylor—"

Calypso's gaze was so white-hot it could have burned a hole straight through her son. She shifted her gaze to Lady. "Yes, I understand. You acted in good faith. I consider your debt paid as fully as if you'd put the Mermaid's Lament into my hands. I shall consider us still good friends."

"Thank you," Lady said, but there wasn't much warmth in her voice.

Calypso returned the harsh glare of her gaze to Saylor, who hung his head.

"Look at me, son."

He slowly raised his head.

"You will return home with me now," the sea goddess said. "I will devise your punishment as we travel."

Saylor gulped but nodded. He waded into the water to await his fate.

And still I had no pity for him.

Calypso faced Lady. "My deepest apologies for my son's behavior."

Lady waved it off with a flick of her hand. "My yard is in ruins. You will, of course, send a crew to repair it and oversee them yourself."

Calypso stared hard at Lady and then dipped her chin in a tiny acknowledgement. "Of course. Tomorrow is acceptable for you?"

Lady nodded her approval.

Calypso turned and walked into the sea.

Outside, a mockingbird sang his midnight serenade, a combination of various songs interspersed with the sound of a car alarm. Lady had gone to bed saying she had an important business meeting in the morning and wanted to be fresh for it. Edwin and I sat in the kitchen unwinding over a couple of beers.

"Will Calypso really show up tomorrow to oversee the workers, or was that just face-saving goddess bullshit?" I asked.

Edwin laughed under his breath. "She'll show up, but she won't stay all day, especially once she learns that Lady isn't even here. She may bring Saylor though and make him stay and probably make him do the cleanup work as well. Probably whatever she decides is the very worst job there is to do." He tipped the bottle to his lips. "Our job will be to get out there at first light and gather all the pearls before the workers arrive."

I glanced at the clock. Getting up at dawn meant I wasn't going to get much sleep, but I was too wound up to simply slip off to bed now.

"Is it true that with the pearls out of order, the spell is broken and can't be recast?"

He gave me one of those '*who knows?*' looks. "They say the sorcerer who cast the spell spent years working it up and refining it. They say he never shared the secret. They say he's dead. If there's a lie in there somewhere, I'm sure Lady will find it. She's very persistent."

"Hence the reason we need to gather all the pearls."

"Yes," he said.

"Then my job is done. Lady hired me to recover the pearls and now—" I turned my palms up in a gesture of finality.

Edwin peered at me over the top of his bottle. "I think she plans to keep you on full-time. Lady appreciates competence."

He must have caught the look the word *competence* inspired.

"More than competent," he said. "Good enough for her to continue to employ you, and she does have exacting standards."

There were questions that had pricked at the back of my mind for a while. This seemed a good moment to have them answered.

"The day of the interviews at Lady's office—were you there playing the demon role? Two demons in fact?"

Edwin shrugged. "I have many talents."

I sipped my beer thinking how true that statement was. I set the bottle on the table.

"Saylor said that your only other form was the dragon," I said. "How did you pull of the demons?"

"Saylor doesn't know everything."

Saylor and I seemed to have that in common. I was sure there was more to this new society I'd fallen into than I knew. Much more.

He smiled. "A good glamour goes a long way."

"Cast by you or by Lady?"

"Lady doesn't have that sort of magic," he said.

A glamour cast by Edwin, whom I hadn't known had that sort of magic? Or by Dr. Sharma, who plainly showed he did have magic? Or a different, outside entity I knew nothing about?

I lifted my bottle and took another sip of beer. I was

keyed up but worn out. Did it matter who had cast the glamour? Nope.

"They're harsh, aren't they? The goddesses," I said.

Edwin shrugged again. "They have their own ways."

I pursed my lips, wondering if I should ask the next question. Did I really want to know?

"You know my house flooded."

"Yeah," he said.

"Did Lady make that happen?"

Edwin shook his head. "Again, she doesn't have that sort of magic. She could probably divert a river if she wanted, but I don't think she can control something manmade like a sewer."

"You don't *think*?"

He shrugged. "You're going to have to ask her directly for a definitive answer."

"So, she might have done it?"

"Might have. Lady tends to get what she wants and doesn't have a lot of qualms about doing what she has to do to get it. As I said, the gods and goddesses have their own ways."

"Okay," I muttered, and let the question go for now.

I watched a drip of condensation roll slowly down the bottle in front of me.

"You know," I said, "the same could be said for you—about having your own ways. You're a demigod and a dragon. I work in the magical world and you're the first person of that combo I've met. First dragonshifter I've met at all. First demigod, for that matter."

"I'm Edwin," he said, looking straight at me. "No different than you're Shay, despite your special abilities."

I thought about that. We might not be *ordin*, but we felt ordinary to ourselves, at least I did. Maybe it was something like being a music virtuoso or a brilliant athlete—a gift of birth you could hone but ultimately simply was who and what you were. Or in my case, a gift handed to me whether I wanted it or not.

"Fair enough," I said, and we fell into a companionable silence.

Thank you for reading *The Mermaid's Lament*. I hope you enjoyed it. If you would be so kind as to leave a short review on Amazon, I would be most appreciative. Click here or type the URL into the address bar on your computer to leave a review: mybook.to/TheMermaidsLament

In book two, *The Goddess Jar*, Shay is on the hunt for a stolen artefact containing the soul of an ancient, evil goddess. Being forced to team up with Saylor even for a minute makes her none too happy, but if she doesn't recover the jar before the thief can pry it open, being teamed with Saylor will be the least of her—and the world's—worries. Get it here: https://books2read.com/u/b55W81

CONTACT INFORMATION

Readers Group: https://www.facebook.com/groups/171907636907430/

Facebook: https://www.facebook.com/AlexesRazevichAuthor

VIP Mailing List: http://eepurl.com/08229

Website: AlexesRazevich.com

Email: LxsRaz@yahoo.com

Bookbub: https://www.bookbub.com/profile/alexes-razevich

Twitter: https://twitter.com/lxsraz

Instagram: AlexesRazevichAuthor

BY ALEXES RAZEVICH

Urban Fantasy

Ice-Cold Death Oona Goodlight, book one
Barbed Wire Heart Oona Goodlight, book two
Vulture Moon Oona Goodlight, book three
Chalice and Blade Oona Goodlight, book four

The Mermaid's Lament Shay Greene, book one
The Goddess Jar Shay Greene, book two

Magic Forbidden Heart Mountain Academy, book one
Magic Freed Heart Mountain Academy, book two

Historical Urban Fantasy

The Girl with Stars in her Hair

Science Fantasy

The Ahsenthe Cycle

Khe, Khe, book one
Ashes and Rain, Khe, book two
Gama and Hest, companion novella
By the Shining Sea, Khe, book three

Contemporary Fantasy

Shadowline Drift

If you'd like to be among the first to know when new books arrive, I'd love for you to sign up for my VIP Readers Group by clicking ***here*** or typing ***http://eepurl.com/80229*** in the search bar. I respect your privacy and would never sell or share your information. As a thank you, I'll gift you a copy of my urban fantasy novella, *Bird Song.*

Made in the USA
Coppell, TX
01 April 2020